SALT CITY

Also by Robert C. Fleet

Heart of Stone
Last Mountain
White Horse, Dark Dragon
Happy New Year

ROBERT C. FLEET

SALT CITY

SALT CITY

Red Frog Publishing is a division of Red Frog Media
112 Harvard Ave. # 43 Claremont, CA 91711.
www.redfrogpublishing.com

First Edition   Literary
                    Fiction/Crime
ISBN – 978-0-9845933-6-1 ISBN - 098-4593365

1   2   3   4   5   6   7   8   9   10

For Alina

Needless to say, all incidents, characters and activities portrayed in this story are fictional. Any resemblance to real persons and incidents is purely coincidental. In addition, most of the locations are fictional, although some – the city of Syracuse, the MONY building, Solvay, Salina Street, Syracuse University and Mobile County, Alabama – I felt were big enough to be flattered by a little dramatization. Besides, this happened so long ago...

RCF

SALT CITY

The "Salt City" is Syracuse, New York. I went to Syracuse University and haven't been back there since. But I was sitting in Krakow, Poland, trying to marry the love of my life, Alina, and the U.S. consul there had also gone to S.U. So, in order to teach Alina English, I began writing a *"criminalky"* using rumored Syracuse scandals that the consul and I both remembered. Alina loved Raymond Chandler - in Polish - and though I'd never read him yet, I tried to fit her descriptions of what she liked. And, because Cold War politics didn't respect love as a reason to stay in a country, there was even a plan to translate my story-for-her into a serialized Polish crime novel so that I could have a visa while waiting for the official docs allowing me to marry Alina. A great plan - until I created a Russian-speaking black detective and people thought I was being politically sarcastic and...

Flash forward a bunch of years... three published novels and six produced screenplays later. (Wish I was rich from that, but life *is* sarcastic.)

Certain characters, certain moral outlooks, stay with you. After *Salt City's* Mark Cornell, I created *Heart of Stone's* Sam Williams. Then, sitting in a temp job in L.A., I brought Sam and Mark together in The *Quiet Child*, a story still unwritten, only outlined. Ten years later I found Sam lamenting Mark's disappearance and wrote *Happy New Year,* adapted into a feature-that-never-happened (typical Hollywood story). Six months later I was sitting in a Carl's Jr., saw a certain waitress delivering my fast food entree, and realized what happened to Mark and Sam in *Broken Doll* (also never written, but understood).

They stay with you. Rereading *Heart of Stone, Salt City* and *Happy New Year*, like my favorite books, I still liked them. They still "mean" something in the current world. "The more things change, the more they stay the same" as the French say. Surprise to me: sad in the overview, pleasant in the "Well, did I have foresight!" ego-world. But each one stands on its own: *Salt City* as the first-born of them all, *Heart of Stone* and *Happy New Year* already out there. Whether the whole family will ever be born, well, we'll see.

RCF

salt city

1977

looking

chapter

one

I felt mean. Not animal mean, like your two-ton football truck drivers, just petty mean. Like that teacher I had in 5th grade, the one who couldn't let a kid go home without at least ten math problems to do and twenty words to spell. Idiot work. I felt that kind of mean that likes to see others waste their time like I am. So I didn't answer right away when the blueshirt asked me what I was doing parked there in the dead of night.

"All right, let's see the license," he said after his fifteen second politeness limit had expired.

This one I knew. Too quick to the pocket and he'd have me out the door and into a body-lock breathing tears: self-defense, "It could have been a gun." Too slow and it was failure to obey an officer's commands. Either way, I'd asked for it. Now, feeling mean, I'd have to eat it. Or lose the twenty-five waiting for me downtown. I like to eat. I went for the money.

"Officer, I'm reaching for my license now," I said, doing just that. "I'm waiting here for my brother-in-law who said to pick him up around one o'clock from his girl's house, only he doesn't want me to ring and so I'm ..." I rattled on, getting worse and worse.

The problem with lying is that you've got to stick to the story. With a good lie, it's no problem. With my lie I'd either better have a brother-in-law show up soon or get a move on and say good-bye to the twenty-five. I felt mean.

Of course, sometimes things work out a third way. It didn't matter who I said was coming once she flew out the window. And once she struck the ground, I couldn't even remember what I'd said.

But sometimes at night I still remember how long it took Anne Malloy to fall those six stories.

chapter

two

Three hours before, Sunday night, Anne Malloy had looked pretty good in the photograph the boss had shown me: tall, thirty and Irish. Perfect little housewife with a touch of life. That was all I knew.

The boss - small, forty and bored - told me to sit outside 210 Salina Street, where I would probably find her bronze Maverick conveniently and foolishly parked, wait there till she came out of the apartment building, take a picture if I could, and tail her discreetly until my shift was up, even if it just meant staring at her house while she slept through the rest of the night. A divorce case. I didn't care. I'm paid twenty-five dollars for eight hours, 10 p.m. to 6 a.m., to follow someone and report what they do. That's all.

That's all I have to do.

That's all I have to know.

That's all that's necessary to wrap up a marriage and deliver it to the divorce courts in New York State this Year of Our Lord, Anno Domini, AD 1977.

I had checked the odometer mileage as I got in my car, I remembered that: at seven cents a mile and thirty cents per half hour of idling time the expenses add up, and I wanted Bill Baeren, alias the boss, to foot the bill whenever and wherever I could put it to him. Then I started out, wondering, but not too much.

What half-hearted speculation I did engage in, in fact, concerned the locale: Salina Street. Salina could be "fun," depending on where in the City of Syracuse I found Number 210. North was white, south was black and 210 was smack in the middle of everyman's land. Which was why the police were quick to question. It was a good area for a little inter-racial robbery.

Only it wasn't a robbery we were watching.

No, we were watching a window six floors up smash open from the impact of a human body. Then that body, a woman's body, dropped down.

I suppose that we expected, the cop and I, to see the body arc through the darkness - hover, perhaps, suspended for a moment in space and time like a swan dive - then gracefully knife through the air into a pool of night. It didn't. When Anne Malloy left solid ground behind her she dropped straight and sprawling. There was no grace to her fall, only time. The slow time that allowed her to let out one sound. And then there was a guard-rail, followed by the ground.

I felt a terrible emotion swell up behind my eyes. I couldn't move. Couldn't. And for a moment the fear that Anne Malloy must have felt took hold of me as I thought of how I would never move. Deep inside something pushed - willed - movement, and I let out a cry to join Anne Malloy's. I pushed against the car door with all my weight, knocking the policeman back as I forced myself out of the car. I ran towards the body. When I got to her, I turned to the nearest bush and vomited. Five seconds later, the policeman joined me at the bush.

* * * * * * * * * *

Police detective Richard Anderson was young, black and lieutenant. He had the kind of eyes I thought they only gave to doctors, the kind that see the symptoms but miss the human bearing them. Only the sweat stains on his clothes betrayed his nerves. It was a cold night.

By the time Anderson arrived I was sitting in my car, idling the engine to keep warm. But the cold was inside me and it didn't want to stop. I thought I'd like to go home and sleep, the wave of adrenaline-drop drowsiness overcoming me unaffected by a pounding heartbeat and racing, frightened emotions.

If I could sleep...

Instead, I sat in my car waiting for the questions to start. I watched the police story outside 210 Salina Street with my windows rolled up, making a silent movie out of the scene: mouths opened and closed, puffs of frosty air hovered in front of every face, policemen and medical examiners walked quickly and businesslike in and out of the apartment building. A black man in maintenance man overalls emerged from the basement of the apartment building, led by two blueshirts. He wore bedroom slippers, and after a moment of observing his possessive gestures and the blueshirts' administrative responses, I realized that he must be the building superintendent.

The silent movie began its second reel: Anderson stood in the middle of it all, practically straddling the body, checking off with a BIC pen something on the clipboard he carried like an extension of his left arm, then using the pen like a baton to waive directions with his right.

My bush became popular with many of the new arrivals.

I thought of turning up the volume, thought better of it, and settled back into a comfortable chill, watching it all through half-closed eyes.

I woke up when he opened the door.

chapter

three

Lieutenant Anderson seemed surprised to find me asleep, then resentful. I looked at him standing there, bending at the waist to poke his head through my passenger-side door. Sweat was beaded on his forehead like an August afternoon.

It was only Monday morning.

Two a.m.

In October.

"Mister? ..."

"Cornell. Mark Cornell."

"Mr. Cornell. I want to thank you, Mr. Cornell. Officer Marron says you helped with the body and-"

"I didn't help," I said abruptly, more upset than I thought I was. "I put my coat over her, that's all. I'm cold."

"It's over there if you want it." It was still across her body.

"I'd rather be cold."

"Yes."

Anderson settled into the seat beside me, keeping his eyes on the activity surrounding the body. The police photographers were finished and the ambulance crew was picking up the pieces for the morgue. Why did they send for an ambulance?, I wondered. Probably 'cause Marron was an optimist.

"You saw the incident?" Anderson asked, his tone indicating it was time for business and that there was really no question in what he had just said.

"Yes" I answered appropriately.

"Let me read this statement," Anderson began, very mechanically. What followed was Officer Marron's account of the fall, essentially the same as mine but with a different imagination filling in the adjectives. Marron had glossed over our little run-in beforehand, either forgetting it or to pay me back for taking care of the body while he'd phoned in. Either way, it didn't matter to Anne Malloy: she was dead whether or not the witnesses to her fall were best buddies or blood enemies. I kept seeing her fall.

I nodded "yes" when Anderson asked if I would corroborate the statement, then I signed the hand-written document in a space big enough for three signatures - if each was the size of a pinhead. I kept seeing her fall.

"That's fine, Mr. Cornell. Thank you very much."

Lieutenant Anderson took the pen from my hand like a teacher gently prying a crayon from a first grader. I guess he was used to dealing with death-stunned witnesses. I was pretty much of a rookie in the field. Anderson's voice matched his touch:

"Of course you'll have to come down to the station tomorrow to make an official statement, but I'll have this one typed and ready and all you'll have to do is drop by my desk and sign it. OK?" As before, Anderson's tone made it clear he was not asking.

"Fine."

"Oh. One last question. You live around here?"

Through my own haze of thoughts about the lady falling, I understood the question enough to stop myself from answering right way. Easy question – should have been an easy answer - but if I told him the truth we would have to start all over again.

I couldn't start all over again. I had to get away from here. I kept seeing her fall.

"No, Lieutenant. I don't live around here. I was waiting for my brother-in-law."

"Fine ... Fine." Anderson paused, looking at the ambulance pull away. He looked cold. He looked like he didn't want to leave my car. I looked down Salina Street and couldn't see a light on that wasn't a streetlight. Or a car. I looked over at Anderson's clipboard. The top page was a grocery checklist, typewritten, ending with a woman's handwriting:

"and You."

* * * * * * * * * *

I'm lucky, I suppose: give me a bed from seven in the morning till one in the p.m. and I can go the next eighteen hours without a break. Not bad unless you've got to work the 9-to-5s. I don't, so I guess I'm pretty lucky. Now I was even more lucky: it was only 4 a.m., Bill Baeren wouldn't be expecting me to call-in till the afternoon, so I could get in three hours off the front.

Try sleeping after a murder.

TV?

Nope. Good ol' Syracuse closes down at one.

Radio?

At this hour only Feelin' Husky (or was it Loretta Livin'?) was wailing the virtues of lost virginity and strong daddies.

Eat.

... Eat?

No. There are some feelings you have to be hungry for. And clean. The ritual kind. Despite the fact that my apartment building actually has a decent supply of hot water, I turned on the cold, ran it over my hands and waited till my fingers felt numb. Then I wiped my hands across my face, shoveling handfuls of liquid ice into my eyes, and rinsed my mouth with the cold clean chemical water. Later, I sat in the only chair I owned, a big comfortable armchair with a high back and thick, padded arms, a chair that I'd found abandoned on the sidewalk.

I wasn't cold now, not even with the window open.

chapter

four

I didn't have to leave the chair to phone Baeren's office. I dialed his private number, the one without the answering machine: I thought Bill himself would like to console me.

His phone only rang once. Another busy Monday.

"Bill?"

"Yeah, Mark?"

I waited. Damn, I wanted *some* consolation.

"You are, without a doubt, one hell of a swell fella," I said after an indecent pause.

"Yeah, I can see that. I'm giving you twenty-five dollars a night to compliment me. Remind me of that when I'm as slow with your paycheck as you are with a report."

Something was missing. Maybe not grief, I didn't expect that, but divorce detectives don't have their clients' wives murdered then go on with the business day without any reaction.

"Did you read the morning papers, Bill?"

"Yeah, why?"

"For Christsake, Bill, Syracuse doesn't have that many murders! Didn't you see it?"

"See wha-"

"She's dead, Bill!" said the high voice. My voice. I stopped.

"Anne Malloy is dead, Bill," I began again, slowly.

Bill Baeren said nothing, so I continued: "I saw her die. Someone threw her out the window of the apartment you sent me to watch. It was a long fall, Bill. Read your paper, it'll be there."

I expected a pause, a rush of "Oh, God!" inhaled breath, then an apology from Bill. Instead I got a the kind of subtexted whine to his voice that says "You're probably bullshitting my time, but just in case -"

"I read the paper, Mark. There's no mention of Anne Malloy." I could hear the nervous rustle of the thin pages. "Here, page two, they write about a window accident, possible suicide, but no names, no addresses."

"The police are probably holding off on the name till they tell the husband," I answered.

I was beginning to feel something sharp in my stomach. I hoped it was hunger.

"Nope. Says here '... no identification. Police are searching for clues to identity ...' et cetera, et cetera."

Baeren paused. I could hear the pages rustle again, only it was a stall this time, not a search. He began making a strange sound that I tried hard not to recognize.

"You didn't tell them anything?" he said at last.

"I corroborated a policeman's statement. We watched her fall."

"And that's all?"

"All."

There was a sigh and a ceasing of the strange sound.

"O.K."

My stomach still felt odd.

"Now listen, Mark, listen good," Baeren suddenly rushed, "I don't know if you know it, but for some reason we got lucky on this one."

I began to realize that it wasn't hunger I felt. Baeren's following speech only confirmed my diagnosis.

"The police don't - I repeat 'Don't' - like private operators. Don't with a capital 'D'. I guess they figure you were just a passerby. That's good. We'll just let them run their investigation without complications, and you can be free of-"

"I've got to go back this afternoon to sign an official statement."

When Bill Baeren is frustrated he sucks in his left cheek and chews it. It hurts me to watch. Right then it was hurting me to hear.

"You already made a statement?"

"A cop saw me parked outside and was asking me questions when she went out the window. I said I was waiting for my brother-in-law."

"And this 'official' statement today: is it supposed to be a new statement?"

"Only if I want. Lieutenant Anderson strongly implied that he'd prefer the statements to stay the same."

"How strongly?"

"It'll be typed and waiting."

Baeren stopped chewing his cheek.

"But they don't even know who she is," I said. "I've got to tell them."

The chewing started again.

There wasn't much to do for the next minute but wait as Baeren continued to masticate his mouth.

I stood up and shambled over to the bookcase; after seven hours in a chair all I could do was shamble. I selected the three books I needed for class that day. One was long and interesting, two were small and deadly. I'd go to the police after Hegel. There was some justice in that. Baeren stopped chewing his cheek:

"Mark, I can't take the publicity. My business doesn't like publicity. The police don't like my business." Bill was being very sincere now, and getting to the heart of his concern - himself.

But I thought about it.

* * * * * * * * * *

I was still thinking about it when Philosophy 501, Hegel and His Times, ended. It was the kind of boring class where thinking about anything but the subject at hand was subliminally encouraged by every word droned.

For me it didn't matter what would happen with "the business" - I'm paid twenty-five dollars a night to follow husbands errant or wives astray and it keeps my afternoons open for the graduate program at Syracuse University. But I had a scholarship, so all I was risking was the loss of a little extra money and a schedule that fit in with my sleep patterns.

Not so for William H. Baeren, Esquire: he was not a thirty-one year-old "professional" student but an unimaginative little lawyer who'd found a way to pull in forty thousand (net) a year without taxing his minimal legal talents. He also owed me three weeks' back pay, a situation guaranteed to deteriorate upon the occurrence of any sudden business reversals.

And so it was with a less-than-decisive step that I entered Police Department, determined to do my duty.

chapter

five

Police Department. The lobby waiting room was large and relatively comfortable: air conditioning (I don't know why it was churning in October, but it was), several couches built to seat four (usually occupied by two strangers disconcerted by the presence of their seat-mates), and a large picture window on either side of the entrance (looking out on the panorama of a tarmac parking lot). The only thing missing was the familiar buzz and strobe effect of a defective fluorescent light. The secretary at the Information Desk seemed becalmed by the oversight.

She was, unfortunately, beautiful.

In addition to black hair parted in the middle and falling exactly to her shoulders, the Info Desk secretary possessed the only nose I have ever seen that looked good supporting black glasses. Those glasses fronted a pale-but-not-too complexion and the most naturally red lips that I had yet known. She wore one of those secretary blouses that button up to the throat and ruffle - only on her I wanted to see the throat.

And she looked at me as if I didn't exist.

This after I stood in front of her station and spoke in what I was assured by my Speech 204 final presentation evaluation (an A-earning performance) is a "strong, clear, decisive voice."

"I'd like to see Detective Lieutenant Anderson," I said.

"He's not at his desk this afternoon." There was a quick look at her register. "I believe he has some-"

"Jeanne, I'll be in the coffee room. I'll sign-in in about fifteen minutes."

So her name was "Jeanne." That established, I turned and used my nascent detective skills to examine the speaker.

The man who was about to be in the coffee room was at least fifty, bald and possessed of a lunar-landscaped face. A detective. An ordinary guy whose wedding ring spoke of a wife and whose shuffling walk mentioned that he was tired to boot. His smile was nice though.

But not as nice as Jeanne's. She turned a look on him that said he was one of the greatest men alive. She smiled just as nicely twice more at a pair of plainclothesmen checking in. Then she turned to me and I didn't exist.

"I believe Lieutenant Anderson left a statement for you to sign," Jeanne said, not really paying attention to where she was looking. It was a really good voice. Not a hint of scrape, screech or Syracuse twang.

I didn't ask for the statement.

"Tell him I'll be back. I have some information that he needs. Some real information."

I started out the entrance. As I pushed the door that said "Pull" I looked back.

Jeanne was writing. I didn't exist.

I wanted that smile.

chapter

six

OK, there are stupid reasons for impulsive actions. But my brain works a little slower than my body sometimes and as I crawled over the city atop elevated highway Route 81 I picked up a few good reasons to keep me from stopping and going right back to the police:

First, Bill Baeren was right - the police were not going to be pleased with my presence complicating their case.

Second, because I hadn't given them what I knew last night, they had just wasted a day's legwork on some half-assed detective's notion that the police know who everybody is. (Still hadn't gotten over the university paranoia of '69.)

Third, i.e., Conclusion: I had better give Anderson something more than I had to offer at present if I wanted my head to remain on my body instead of on a silver platter.

So, Jeanne of the Syracuse Police Information Desk, though I wanted your smile, hoped for your love and would have settled like a dog for your merest attention, you were only the impetus, not the reason, to get me off my butt.

I headed for Solvay. According to the work order Bill Baeren had worked up for me, the town of Solvay was where Anne Malloy had a house address. On my own I filled in a probable two cars. And, of course, a husband who had hired the law firm of William H. Baeren, Esq. to obtain the evidence necessary to prove a divorce case based on adultery.

Husband's name: Davis Malloy. In the work order.

Syracuse is not a big city, area-wise. Settled in a valley, you can walk from one skyline to another in an hour. You can drive through it in about an hour, too (thanks to uncoordinated stoplights, one-way streets and poor road planning), or you can drive over it, on 81, in fifteen minutes, missing anything that's worth living there for and catching only the tar-paper and grey-metal rooftops. The highway splits over James Street, North and West, then splits again over a street I can never remember till I've missed it. This time, headed for Solvay, I didn't have to worry: for some reason Solvay gets well-marked on the road signs.

Solvay is separated from Syracuse by Lake Onondaga, an airport, and the processing plants that give Syracuse its nickname, "The Salt City". Lake Onondaga has a saline content triple that of the other thousand lakes of upstate New York: lousy for fishing, great for industry.

Beyond the factories is a vague area that I've never paid enough attention to to describe. It's a half-hearted tract of woods or old fields or some of both. This trip it was October and brown-yellow, separating housing developments in Syracuse from housing developments in Solvay. I think there was another town in-between. I don't know. When I go on vacations it's not to there.

Davis Malloy would be at 59 Emma Drive.

I liked their house.

The grass was a little worn, like when kids play around on it a lot. There was a broken window pane taped over with cardboard up on the second floor. The room behind that window was wall-papered in a children's print, tasteless and full of kids' dreams. The garage was open - and clean, something I found hard to believe until I saw how precariously ordered everything was. I gave it two days till tools were cluttering up the driveway and sawdust would be shuffling round the floor. As I walked to the front door I began to feel comfortable.

Then I remembered why I was there. I liked their house. I was going to foul it up.

No one answered the doorbell.

I wasn't very surprised. While I'd been rhapsodizing the Malloy's habitat I had also noticed that there were no cars near the house, excepting mine, and no lights on inside. I didn't wonder where the kids were: when parents are on the outs with each other kids have a way of getting themselves invited to friends' homes for dinner. Or relatives'.

Nobody home.

Maybe Davis Malloy was working late a few minutes. It was only five-thirty, I could wait. I'm good at waiting. People pay me for it. I could do a freebie. I headed for my car.

I slipped a cassette into the portable tape-recorder I keep locked up in the glove compartment, sat back into the corner behind the steering wheel, and played silent movie again.

The cassette was an old one, a home-made recording of me playing the flute, back in my Music Major year. Berio's "Sequenza". Sparse, trilling flute (I wasn't bad when I practiced), lacking a piano accompaniment (I just didn't like the piano) - scraping sounds on the dusk.

It was a bad choice of music, making my friendly house turn hollow and haunted. No one came home.

I played the cassette again. I went to a movie and laughed. I liked the movie a lot. An awful lot. I like laughing. I get bored with myself when I play serious too long. After two hours I had jollied up and was headed back to the Malloys'.

Still no one: no man, no kids, no lights. It was nine o'clock.

I'm not a real detective: I don't know how to improvise beyond a certain point, I just do Bill Baeren's night snooping for him. The easy kind: with a notebook, a camera and my eyes. Real or pseudo, it struck me that I'd let the time slip by and gotten in deeper with Lieutenant Anderson's eventual wrath. I'd better get something for him as a peace offering.

I couldn't leave a note for Davis Malloy, not with the information I had elected to deliver to his doorstep. I looked at the neighbors' houses. I couldn't even tell them apart. No, there were small differences: red shutters here, a bicycle there, a Halloween goblin already up - tributes to the small battle of the individual to break out. But not enough. Not enough for me at any rate to go there and ask for help. None would be individual enough to take a man at his word coming out of the dark. I would get nothing from these houses, even if they knew.

Then I noticed: the Malloy's garage was now closed. Someone had been back to the house – and left.

I looked around again, taking a side of the house blind to the neighborhood and looking in the windows. No sign of a break-in. Someone had come back home and closed the garage and, knowing kids, I was pretty certain it had been the Dad.

I headed for the Sip 'n Sit two blocks over.

chapter

seven

It doesn't take an idiot to figure out that a man whose wife has been gone for almost two days might possibly decide to seek solace with the jolly company of his fellows. I knew the routine from my own family, even though Mom never disappeared. If you were a guy, you had to go to a bar sometimes. Just to talk - even if, like Dad, you didn't talk. You just had to do it. I guess that's what separated our generations. I never felt the obligation. But, hell, I can sit at home and not talk just as well and for half the price. I'm cheap.

Sip 'n Sit had a 5-to-6 cocktail hour, nice buffet, and from what I could smell a pretty good recipe for chili. It also had lots of alcohol, a bunch of five drinking heavily of that alcohol, and Davis Malloy in the middle of that bunch, buying.

It was not the situation to intrude upon.

I was made to recognize Davis Malloy as the

result of a matter-of-fact statement: the bartender was tallying up a bill as I entered and before I could order my own "thinking-out-the-problem" drink, he'd presented it to a thin-haired man saying, "Here you are, Mr. Malloy." Luck was with me. Some luck. As I ordered my drink I decided to sip 'n sit 'n see 'n hear.

What Solvay couldn't give Malloy, age was: an aura of dignity. Thirty-five to forty-five years old, I couldn't tell, a receding hairline and deep blue eyes graced Davis Malloy with a caring look sans pretension: he wasn't trying to look any way. My height, maybe broader. I knew he was as much unaccustomed to drinking as a water buffalo. (Bill Baeren digs up a little dirt on both parties, in case he has trouble bill collecting - something about "the truth will out, though not in court.") All the same, Davis Malloy looked cold sober and, well, justified. He wasn't buying bravado, he was simply paying his turn. Malloy's friends, each of whom must have had his own night, drank solemnly, talked out. They were a wall to keep his emotions in and others out. Others like me. I was stalemated for an hour.

Gradually, however, they began to leave. First two, twenty minutes later one, then the last pair. They asked Malloy if he wanted a lift.

"No. Car's outside." Slight drawl, but regional, not drunk. Southern. Davis Malloy was not a local boy from "Seer-accuse."

I edged myself over along the bar till I was within talking distance for the quiet night and waited to catch his eye. Five, ten minutes. He wasn't going to raise his eyes from the peanut bowl, much less turn them in my direction. He laid a twenty dollar bill on the counter and kept his eyes on the peanuts. When the bartender swept up the twenty and didn't lay down another drink, I knew that the tab was paid. Davis Malloy would be leaving sooner than later. So I made a mistake.

I approached Malloy with the kind of introduction that needs a crowded bar and a bowl of pretzels: it was too obvious, too big and too noisy for the situation. I walked over, reached across Malloy for a napkin, and plopped down in the seat next to him. His eyes shifted from the peanuts to my hands on the bar cradling my long-nursed whiskey sour. His body language, according to a new Psych course I was taking, said that he was annoyed by the intrusion upon his "space." He had a right to be annoyed. If Davis Malloy didn't like me now, he'd think I was a hell-of-a fella in a few minutes.

"Mind if I sit here?" I friendlied.

"No."

He stood up and walked out the door.

I turned to the bartender, trying to look innocent and bewildered. It felt phony as hell from the inside, but it got me a piece of information I couldn't have bought.

"You didn't say anything," the bartender said, replenishing the peanut bowl and evaluating my neglected whiskey sour with a practiced eye that knew I wasn't buying more. "He had a death in the family."

I already knew that. I decided to upset the bartender's expectations and loosen his tongue by sliding two dollars across the bar and overpaying for a Coke. "Help me pretend it's a real drink," I kidded and he nodded back with a smile. The smile was good - again, according to my Psych class - it meant he could be opened up. I needed more information on the Malloy family.

"Yeah," I said, "too bad about that guy's family. Anybody close?"

"His kid. Died Saturday, of cancer."

Too bad I didn't want that information.

chapter

eight

I decided to stop playing detective. I wasn't going to tell Davis Malloy about his wife, I'd let Anderson have that pleasure. I headed for the Police Department and the chewing out I deserved. It was almost eleven by the time I arrived there, so I figured the overnight shift would be going full swing.

Reprieve time: no Detective Lieutenant Anderson.

Another reprieve: as expected, Jeanne of the Beautiful Smile was off-duty for several hours and another secretary manned the Information Desk, so I signed the prepared statement without incident or injury to ego. The secretary let me know that the lieutenant should be in about midnight, did I care to wait? Did I have a message? I answered politely "no" to both inquiries and beat a hasty retreat. Tonight, Anderson was going to receive one of those famous "anonymous tips" phoned-in to him about midnight, a tip that would lead him to Solvay and a house with worn grass. Maybe he would have time to visit the Sip 'n Sit before it closed. I went home and started to watch The Tonight Show. It wasn't as much fun since Johnny Carson moved the show from New York to Los Angeles a couple of years ago, but it was still Johnny.

Bill Baeren telephoned at eleven-thirty-five, right in the middle of Johnny's comic monologue. That was the best part of the show and now I had to listen to Baeren chewing his cheek again.

"Mark? I didn't hear from you today. What happened?" I thought of raw hamburger.

"Nothing, Bill. The guy wasn't in, the police lieutenant. I signed the statement he wrote up for me, that's all." I tried to still listen to Johnny's monologue and use the distraction to leave out telling Baeren my plans for the future; my cheeks were hurting in sympathy for the guy. "That's all, Bill."

"Christ, Mark, that's good -"

I started reading the titles in my bookcase as Baeren sighed his own long monologue about luck and intelligence in my ear. Vaguely, between the mix-match of Johnny's and Bill's competing monologues, I realized that I was getting more intelligent by the minute until, finally, Baeren concluded with, "- well, we can't call it full time, but if you get a move on I can get you a few hours in tonight."

Johnny's monologue was finished, too, and I wasn't close to falling asleep.

"Thanks, Bill."

"Did you get the address?"

"No."

He repeated it.

The moment I put the receiver down I remembered. I dialed Baeren's number.

"Bill?"

"All right! Full time credit!"

"*Merde* the full time. What did you tell Davis Malloy?"

"Christ, Mark, forget it!"

"Don't 'Christ' me, Bill, I-"

"You're not gonna-"

"- I want some decency here. I gotta know."

"Know what?"

"What you, William Baeren, attorney, told your client, Davis Malloy, about what happened to his wife, Anne Malloy, dammit!"

"Nothing!"

There was a pause while I tasted the dirt in my mouth. Baeren, obviously, was used to the flavor.

He also took my pause of confusion to be some sort of definitive statement from me and took up the argument with his own heat:

"Listen, Cornell, you want to work for me, fine!, only don't... don't play detective!"

"I didn't call the guy up, that's what I told him. He didn't call me up. If he does, I'll find a way to be out. Believe it or not, I know when to take a business loss - I'm not going to call Davis Malloy up and present my bill. I'm not gonna call him up period!"

Baeren halted in mid-anger, then muttered as much to himself as to me:

"He'll know soon enough."

Will he?, I thought, or will he still be thinking about his dead son? It was not a thought I planned on sharing with Bill Baeren. Not that I was planning anything at this point. But I sure as hell wasn't telling him anything.

I needed fresh air and Bill Baeren might as well pay for it.

"Give me tonight's address again, Bill. I forgot to write it down."

Half an hour later I was in DeWitt, another town outside of Syracuse, sort of rich. Nice rolling hills. On the top of one of those hills I found a police call box. I telephoned Lieutenant Anderson.

He still wasn't in yet. I left him a cryptic message and Malloy's address, and left a dime in the call box. Then I returned to my car and went home - the husband who'd told his wife he was "working late" had already left "work." I didn't get a photo, an out-the-door time, or even arrive in DeWitt in time to confirm that his Caddy had been parked anywhere near the probable liaison address. Bill Baeren would be pissed.

I already was.

chapter

nine

I don't sleep very well between one a.m. and seven, but I sleep. By eight o'clock Tuesday morning I had eaten. By nine o'clock I was playing detective again. I had one thing, one little card, that I hadn't told anybody about.

And it was, literally, a card. A business card - of sorts. The card had been lying in Anne Malloy's face when I'd put my coat over its memory. She'd been holding the small rectangle of thin cardboard, I imagined, when her left hand became a part of her face. People will hold on to anything when falling. Sometimes it keeps you from hitting the ground.

I'd kept the card, absently at first, then...

I don't know why. I'd kept it; now I was playing a hunch. I drove down to 210 Salina Street.

I don't look like a detective, or a cop, and I don't have the imagination to risk fake credentials. So when the building superintendent answered his door I told him I worked for the Syracuse Star. It was an easy lie, since the qualifications to be a news stringer for the Star pretty much matched my skills: find a story, type it up. I type.

It used to be that superintendents were of two sorts: old craftsmen or old drunks. Now managements shoot for the young married type who needs an apartment for free, can fix a sink and can dial a phone for the bigger problems. My man looked like he might have trouble fixing a sink, but could dial a phone in a breeze.

In fact, I figured he could take the phone apart in a breeze, build a new one, or re-wire the whole city: as he opened his door, the sight that greeted me was a room spider-webbed full of electrical equipment and wiring. When we spoke it was a conversation paced by the super's eyes looking more interested in the batteries of my watch than in my prose.

I asked the typical prelims.

"Who rents the apartment?"

"No one. Unoccupied." He wasn't any more wary than a wild cat.

While we talked sweet nothings, though, the white-palmed hand holding a screwdriver reflexively tightened, untightened, retightened a screw on a door hinge. The middle one, middle screw. That would have been annoying - except that my peripheral attention was on the man's other, dark brown hand, unconsciously clenched. Tight.

"And who had access to keys to the apartment?" I asked in what I hoped was a routine, by-the-numbers voice.

"Me'n the management."

He tested the swing of the door. It hadn't made a sound before, it didn't now, but I enjoyed the performance.

"You know," he added, "it's not difficult to break into a room."

"And you were..."

"With my wife..."

"And the management is..."

"A real estate company..."

I liked our rhythm, it reminded me that better men than I had probably asked the same questions thrice as many times in the past two days.

I showed him the card.

He didn't like the card.

"Damn Ray!" was his first response, after he'd stared at it for a minute. Then he stared at it again.

Then he looked at the blood on the card.

Then he gave it back.

"Damn Ray!"

"I believe that's a possibility," I said, pleased at the sound of it. "Is your wife home?"

He held the door wider and I stepped in. No doubt about it: plumber-superintendents were an apartment-a-dozen, electrician-supers had to be sought and bought. Only - why bother? We were on Salina Street not Park Avenue. The money some people throw around.

We placed ourselves in folding chairs on diagonal ends of a workbench.

"Who did you say was the management?"

"E.S.T.O."

"E.S.T.O. Real Estate?"

His finger tapped a certificate taped onto the wall. "Eastern States Title Operators is what it stands for."

Eastern States Title Operators - E.S.T.O. Fine. They also owned my apartment building and two or three dozen housing developments. Except my building supervisor couldn't fix a light bulb. I was jealous.

"Ray?" he asked, bursting my bubble of reverie.

I looked at the card I had given him and he had given me back. The card found on Anne Malloy's body. A small white business card, with the typewritten self-advertisement:

I am Ray. A lover-man.
I am good for women.
I am good for you. You
see me and you see a
goodthing. You see me
and you see my eyes.
You see me and you see
LOVE.Love, sister.

I began to read it aloud, with only a faint trace of embarrassment to my voice. The super (I still hadn't asked his name) looked at my knees.

"Fuckin' St. Johns," he groaned.

I held on to the name. "Ray St. Johns."

When I'd finished reading, I sat back, looked at the blood smearings on Ray St. Johns' business card and said, "Well?"

"He had a key."

"Long?"

"Six months. I 'owed' him a night."

"Six months is longer than a night."

"The crazy brother never gave it back. He gets in there sometimes, but gets out before I can know it."

"He do this a lot?" I was falling into the super's way of talking, unconsciously I think, but it was helping him open up to the white boy and I didn't stop.

The super spat out an angry grin. "Only three, four times. Ray's smart enough not to push his luck with me."

"That night?"

Eyes piercing mine, searching for trust. I guess he found it.

"Yeah."

No, there would be no reason for him to trust me. "How do you know?" I said, adding a slight push to my voice.

"I know."

"How?"

"I kn-"

"How?!"

I was glad he answered then, before I started playing movie Indian.

"I know what the room looks like after Ray-" his embarrassment was unfaked, "Ray's- got a woman. I saw the room before that night, and I had to clean it up after. I know he was there."

"With Anne Malloy?"

He looked at me, eyes searching my face for the first time.

He was hearing her name for the first time, too.

"You know who she was?"

I didn't want questions about myself; I already knew my track record for lying to the police. I pressed him. "I'm asking about Ray St. Johns."

That shook him a little more. I didn't think he'd remember saying the name.

I knew I could press still more: "What do you know?"

"He... he was there with a woman, I know that. Not her, Anne...?"

"Malloy."

"Somebody else. She - th'other one - musta left first, they always do." The super started rambling and I let him, not quite sure what I wanted to ask next and hoping he'd lead me there. "I caught him once - Ray, y'know, alone - and he laughed about it, about havin' a woman sneak away from a man's bed, and, y'know ... She, that Annie, she came later."

So that's what I wanted answered:

"Were they together? Ray and - Annie?"

"I don't know." The super thought about his answer, looking at his own white-palmed, black-fingered hands as he concluded: "I didn't think Ray made it with white women."

"She was with him."

"I don't know that."

"She had his card."

"I don't know! I was asleep! I do that, y'know!"

I walked over to the telephone, found the directory sitting underneath it and leafed through to "St. Johns". (A moment of panic: would it be under "Sa" or "St"? I'd feel extremely stupid if I couldn't find any St. Johns.)

"Forman Street?" I asked.

I knew it was, there was an ink mark next to it. I didn't wait for an answer. I picked up the telephone.

"Since you appear to have an aptitude for wiring," I said, "I don't believe this will inconvenience you too much." With that I yanked the telephone and pulled the wire from the wall. "I'd like to visit Ray unannounced."

As I walked out the door I saw the superintendent move towards the kitchen and the second extension. I still hadn't remembered to ask his name; I guess I wouldn't be able to refer to him as a reference. He hadn't thought to ask my name, either. We were both pretty sloppy about this whole business.

Inexperience shows, I suppose.

chapter

ten

I didn't have to worry about the superintendent calling Ray St. Johns to warn him about my coming. Forman Street was close enough to be there in five minutes. Ray St. Johns was tired enough to let his phone ring without touching it.

It was ringing as I walked up the steps of the two-floor apartment building. I waited outside his door while it rang: somebody was inside, shuffling about, I could hear that. Someone picked up the receiver, stopping the ringing, then set the receiver down again, having raised it no more than an inch off the phone.

I knocked on the door, picked up the plastic '21' that fell off of it, put it back on its nail, held it there with my left hand and knocked again with my right.

"In, brotheh," came mumbling through the door. I waited. No sound. Then "In, brotheh!" again. The emphasis was pure sleep. The door was unlocked.

I walked in.

Ray St. Johns apparently had not moved from the telephone. He was standing next to it in a lazy 'S' slouch, staring at a spot of nothing somewhere in the space in front of his face. Not at the floor, though his eyes were cast in that direction - he was too sleep-dazed to see that far.

Army boxer shorts and an Army T-shirt, black socks, five-ten, hundred and fifty/sixty pounds, lean face, lean hands, skinny, Genghis Khan eyes with a moustache to match: Ray St. Johns, alias "a lover-man", was still wearing his hair net. Which was OK, since it didn't bother either of us.

He pointed to a sofa-bed, I sat on it, and he moaned his way towards an open door behind the entrance, the bathroom. He started to pull down his shorts, looked over at me, then closed the door. I appreciated the gesture.

I leaned back against a convenient wall and looked around. There wasn't much to say about the apartment: it had everything you'd need, if you had another apartment to hop off to sometimes. It didn't really interest me very much. I'd lived in worse, but not much, and I was living in better, but still not much. I liked his stereo equipment, I didn't like his decor - early boot-camp macho, centering around the framed photograph of a not much younger Technical

Sergeant Raymond St. Johns. I heard the knocking on the door, heard the '21' fall off it again, and without thinking I stood up and opened it.

There were two of them: one my size, but heftier, wearing a black jacket and a moustache I envied, the other one decked out in brown, with the same facial arrangement, but larger - I like my blaxploitation movies as much as the next guy and this was surely John Shaft and his big brother. I would have sworn to it if the police had asked. The police never asked, so I didn't tell them. 'Shaft' smiled, a friendly smile that I trusted. His 'brother' didn't.

"Hi, Ray in?" Nice voice.

I'm not sure whether I let them in or they walked in on their own, all I knew was that they were inside and I was closing the door by the time Ray St. Johns shuffled out of the bathroom.

Seeing Ray, Shaft-man's smile grew even friendlier. Then bigger. Then deadlier. Shows what kind of judge of character I am.

"You fuckin' St. Johns! What's this shit with you an' my woman last night! Huh, brother! Huh!" Shaft-man went rocketing towards St. Johns while I stood like a spectator, still holding the doorknob.

St. Johns didn't even appear to be awake. He did not react. I couldn't tell if he was faking it or not.

Act or not act, he turned aside just in front of the charge and headed to his left, towards a half-kitchen. Shaft-man stopped in mid-stride, turned, looked at the kitchen, expecting some give-back and, getting zero in return, uncertain what to do next. There was an awkward silence. St. Johns filled a plastic yogurt cup with water. It was the only sound.

"Listen, St. Johns," the charge was on again, "you don't take my woman from me at no party like that!" He grabbed St. Johns by the arm. "And you don't take her to no second party and drop her for no other woman!"

St. Johns said nothing. He waited until his arm was released, then drank his water. Half-asleep, he seemed to wander through the next minute of alternating verbal abuses and silences. I finally let go of the doorknob.

"Es-telle don't mess around with other men 'less they get her drunk," threw in the tall one during one of the pauses.

Shaft-man's pauses were getting fewer and fewer as he kept repeating the story, variated by new obscenities, directly into St. Johns' face: "took my woman, dropped her, took his woman, what'd you do with her?!, took two women in one night!, good women, mother, good, don't mess around" into his face, into his ear.

I sat down on the corner of St. Johns' sofa-bed. It made a sound.

There was another pause. Shaft-man looked at me.

Then the tall one, standing by the stereo, jumped down to a pile of records on the floor.

"These are my records! I gave them to Es-telle!"

All eyes turned on St. Johns.

His face tried to move, tried to break out of its sleep-mask. "I ... I don't know, brotheh," He mumbled.

It wasn't much, but finally getting an answer from St. Johns seemed to resolve something for the two wronged men. They started piling the stolen records into their arms.

When they were finished, Shaft-man turned to St. Johns and glared, "You're no brother, Ray, you're shit!" Then, unexpectedly, they charged out of the apartment.

St. Johns stumbled over to the door, closing it on their footsteps echoing down the stairwell. Through his sleep-mask an easy grin curled out and turned itself on me: "Thanks, brotheh."

I leaned forward from my seat, an apology on my lips, "I thought they were your friends, or I wouldn't have opened..."

"They friends all right," his grin getting more comfortable. "They friends who want to beat the shit out of Ray, but don't like it when he's got a back-up."

Me?

I thought of John Shaft and his big brother. I thought of two-on-one, I thought of two-on-two. I thought of how much I liked the shape of my nose.

I stood up quickly, looking like a guilty schoolboy, caught. St. Johns didn't give it a thought, instead he re-took his sofa-bed from under me. "She was a good woman, Es-telle. Should have stayed, though. Could have gotten a ride to work."

I stood like a clown: "When'd she go?"

"Twen'y minutes ago."

I looked out the window. Two guys, carrying records, were looking at a red Volkswagen. They seemed unsure about something.

"Still in the Army?" I asked.

"Reserves. Got back from Europe year back. Frankfurt. I'm gonna go back to sleep in a minute: close the door behind, OK?"

"Do you know Anne Malloy?"

Nothing.

"Irish woman?"

Nothing.

"210 Salina Street?"

Nothing.

"Do you know that your car needs a new battery?"

"What?" St. Johns started to raise his head, but it was too much effort to ask what I was talking about. He eased back down into his sleep, sighing an answer to my earlier questions. "Brotheh, you know people know where I been."

"So do I."

The sleep-mask faced me.

As I closed the door, the plastic '21' crunched underfoot. I picked it up and put it back on its nail. It wobbled and fell. I slid it under the door. Walking down the steps I let my finger glide across the wall. The crinkle of crackling paint machine-gunned through the stairwell. I stayed on the right side of the stairs, avoiding the curve in the middle of each step. Someone had left the door to the apartment building open. Wind drafted through the halls.

I guessed it was left open by the two guys - John Shaft and his big brother - busy taking the battery out of a red Volkswagen, the one with the West German tourist sticker on it.

chapter

eleven

I attended classes that Tuesday afternoon with a vengeance: firing questions at professors, demanding justifications, overpowering theses - playing the boor successfully enough, I hoped, that they would remember my presence at grade time and be grateful for my studied silence until then. I planned to sleep a lot for the next few weeks.

Anyway, I was angry.

At the same time, I enjoyed exercising the brain instead of the buttocks, as I had of late. I remembered why I was still a student and not "out in the world". "The pursuit of knowledge" had inspired me at one time, still could on occasion. All that was necessary was a little self-discipline. I began to dust off thoughts about shooting for the Ph.D.

Then I thought of Anne Malloy and started to cry.

I don't know why I cried or for how long. It started with a thought, then my face was wet. I was walking through the center of the campus, along the Quad, with tears streaming down my cheeks, embarrassed. I fought the desire to attack the first idiot that came in my way. Instead, I started running towards The Hill, a set of dormitories a quarter of a mile up a hill. (Ha! What an original nickname!) Almost straight up. One hundred fifty-four steps up. Tears smearing across my face and wanting to hit, I ran up. Not breathing, sobbing. Wishing I wasn't so scared.

'Cause that's what it was - I was scared: I wasn't good anymore. I wasn't innocent anymore (hell of a self-pity!), I was alone, I wanted help...

Just like Anne Malloy.

Her face...

Was only a memory from a night.

I stopped running and took out her photograph, the one Bill Baeren had given me: tall, thirty and Irish - perfect little housewife with a touch of life. I looked at the picture a long time. I began to imagine details.

Or notice them.

There was the house. Behind her, the garage, cleaned-up precariously just as I'd come across it.

I wondered if the Polaroid camera had done her justice. Looked like an interesting shot: touch of interest to the eyes, not much of a smile, though. Never get good smiles when you have people pose. Her hair looked fiery against the yellow-brown leaves of October, though her dress was -

October.

I was leaning against a railing at the top of the steps. I had been hot when I'd stopped, hot and wet, my mouth tasting like sweat. I had needed the cool breeze that pointed itself at the back of my neck.

Now the cool breeze was developing daggers and pricked my spine with an uncomfortable cold, like taking an ice cube and running it up and down your back.

The photograph.

A garage.

Cleaned-up precariously...

I thought maybe I'd head back down The Hill, find my car parked along one of the campus side streets where the time limit was short but enforcement lax, and tool over to visit a certain police detective. We had some things to discuss.

My legs couldn't take the stairs. Too rubbery. Fall down The Hill? - Yes. Walk down? - No. I had done things to my muscles running up those one hundred fifty-four steps that only three days' penitence would absolve. I hobbled unsteadily back up, to the opposite direction I wanted to go, to the top, and headed for the dormitories.

Polaroid.

Flagging down a co-ed driving a Mustang, I whined a ride down the long driveway, to be replaced by her boyfriend at the bottom of The Hill. By then my muscles had cramped up enough so that I could hardly walk the flat surfaces. And there was still another hill in-between. It took me thirty minutes and two rides to travel the half mile to where my car was parked.

Slowly and spastically, in deference to calves that had no sympathy for the necessities of coordinating braking with the shifting of gears, I made my way towards the Police Department. I needed some questions asked.

On the way I thought of adulterous wives.

Adulterous wives who wear black armbands.

chapter

twelve

Today was the third Tuesday in October. Two weeks and one day since the Supreme Court had opened session. One week and three days before Halloween. Forty-two hours and twelve minutes since Anne Malloy's death. I had missed Detective Lieutenant Richard Anderson, the man in charge of investigating her murder, three times. I did not miss him on the fourth attempt.

Bending muscle-stiff ankles that didn't want to be bent and knees that actively fought to remain straight, I ached into the Police Department in time to miss my heart's desire of a police secretary on her coffee break. Her official cardboard told me to wait five minutes, but my ego thought it better not to reveal my crippled gait to her critical eye. (I was, after all, only a civilian - not one of her precious detectives.) Instead, I aimed down the left hall and promptly walked past Anderson as he exited the building.

Against all better judgment, I shifted foot gears into a fast jog, catching up with him fifty yards later.

If I had been preoccupied with pride when passing him, Anderson was immersed in other thoughts, so that it wasn't my calling his name but, rather, the labored hop, skip and jog that I used for the last few yards that caught his attention. He looked at me much as a man would who sees a kangaroo ambling down the street. It wasn't until I'd panted out "... the lady in the window..." that his eyes showed signs of recognition.

"Mister...?"

"Cornell. Mark C-"

"Cornell," he cut me off sharply.

Then he looked at me, as if other words were playing at the edge of his thoughts, but said instead with cold precision: "I'm going to work now, Mister Cornell. You go off to yours."

"Sergeant, um, Lieutenant Anderson -" Two can play the snide inference game; it came naturally after student teaching for a semester, "- I came to talk about my statement."

Anderson wasn't playing a game, though. His eyes lit up angrily:

"What statement, Mister Cornell? The one that tells about divorce diggers? Or the one that tells about widowers with dead kids? Or what more have you got ready to talk about?"

He recognized me now.

The only thing in my favor was pain.

Brow-beating me is not difficult: I can be pushed around. But once every six months I blow up. Sometimes not big, sometimes not small. Usually the issue is insignificant, but a line is crossed, a line I hadn't even noticed till then, and I resist. Strongly. Once I'd impressed a girl by taking down an all-hands ski instructor. Twice I'd lost good meals and money defending my "rights" to a substitution in menu. Now I took on Anderson simply because I was in pain from running and didn't want to hear any voice but my own sound self-righteous.

"Shove it, Lieutenant."

I could tell our conversation was going places.

chapter

thirteen

Anderson grabbed me by the left triceps, in the soft spot just above the elbow, and started walking me towards the Police Department entrance.

"All right, Mister Cornell," he whispered, "let's put this on the record again!"

I pulled loose - I didn't like that kind of forced walk - but through the pain in my legs I kept pace with him. We walked silently and smoldering. Fast. Anderson hit the door first with me on his heels. Fast. Fast enough to make eyes follow us down the hall. Fast enough to make co-workers come to Anderson's assistance.

"I'll take care of this!" he shot out, not stopping, as we passed down a hall, through a room full of littered desks, into a file room empty of people - if not of cabinets, a table and several chairs. Anderson went straight to a corner cabinet, pulled it open to where he knew something was, then turned and flung a manila folder at me.

"Thank you, Mr. Cornell, for your statements and your anonymous telephone calls."

I started at the papers in my hand: two of them had my signature and one of them bore my words.

"Let's see, where should we begin, mister divorce detective?" Anderson raced through the sarcasm. "Should I ask you again: 'Why were you there?'...? I've already got your employer's statement about moonlighting. And I've got yours about waiting for a brother-in-law. Two times I've received that little message."

He paused, thinking about that one for a while. I thought about how simple he'd made it for me to agree to those statements. I could see that he was thinking about that, too.

"Why - didn't - you," he slowed down, "make it a clean statement? Now I've got an officer's statement corroborated by just enough contradiction to make it muddy in the courts." He paused again, debating. "And if you think we can just wipe the slate clean and start over again, ..."

I stayed silent. Anderson took the folder and papers out of my hands. He was not aggressive about it.

"In the courts..." he repeated himself. Then his eyes search my face for what he hoped would be a final answer. "A woman commits suicide, or maybe is murdered: it was impossible to tell from your angle."

"I could tell."

"Officer Marron couldn't."

"He was looking at me when she went out the window - I was looking at the window. I could tell the difference between a jump and a shove."

"He says he thinks so, too, but he's not talking facts. Do you know how many unidentified women commit suicide? Do you know how many unidentified women are murdered?" Anderson looked at my textbooks. I hadn't put them down in two hours.

"Not very many," he answered his own question, "not very many of either."

"Davis Malloy." I said simply.

Anderson snapped out of what little professional reflection he was allowing himself. He was angry again.

"I don't have proof it was you, but people saw you there, at the bar, saw you near him."

"It- she was his wife."

"How do you know? How do you know, mister toy detective?! You go searching around and pick the first thing that comes to you? Just because the man rented the apartment for a conference room a month before, did that make him a connection?"

Anderson looked in my face for confirmation. I knew something was showing in my face, I guess he took it for confirmation. "Yes, we check on who rents apartments, too. You know what I spent today doing?"

He didn't wait for an answer.

"I drove seventy-five miles out-of-town to see a man who had rented an apartment at 210 Salina Street for a one-day conference a month ago, and who, by some strange coincidence, was the subject of an anonymous tip saying that this man's wife had been killed.

"This man, as chance would have it, lives in Solvay, but was visiting some property he owns, a nice wooded area, to be alone. He'd buried his son, you see, just this morning. He'd buried his wife, you see, four years ago. He wanted to be alone. He didn't need me. Why don't you go now, Mr. Cornell, and shove it."

I didn't feel bad this time. I didn't feel dirty. I didn't know what the hell was happening, but I knew, finally, that something was. Even as Anderson was turning his back on me, dismissing my existence, I knew that something was.

I left Anderson putting away his file. I didn't even give him the pleasure of seeing me angry: I wasn't - I had questions to ask. I didn't have time to be angry.

Jeanne the Info Desk Queen was back at her place as I walked through the lobby. She'd changed her hairstyle, tousling it into a black mane reminiscent of a certain television star's tresses. She looked more beautiful than before. She also looked like every third beautiful woman in America who was copying the Farrah Fluff. Which made it easy to stop loving her. My wife had looked like Jane Fonda for years and we haven't been on speaking terms since '72 when the divorce papers were signed. I believe in precedent.

I hobbled past her desk. "'Night, Jeanne," I said.

She looked at me and I didn't exist.

chapter

fourteen

Bill Baeren was not happy to see me.

"This is my home, Mark. I don't take business into my home," he whined from his doorstep.

"Where did you telephone me from last night, then, Bill?"

He didn't answer.

He didn't let me inside, either.

Bill Baeren is not a big man. He couldn't be imposing if he tried. When he stepped back into his hallway, slipped on some outdoor clothes, then stepped out to join me in the street, his five-foot, five-inch frame was elevated into a more impressive five-eight, but he was still far from impressive.

What Bill Baeren majored in was the business-like personality, the kind akin to a funeral director's demeanor - efficient, not too pushy, and someone you don't meet for drinks after shop hours.

It was after shop hours now. It was 9:30 at night, a crisp night for walking. We were walking away from Baeren's house and down one of the half-hills separating middle-class Syracuse from the old genteel, towards the Three Palms Restaurant. It was also a bowling alley.

Baeren walked - I hobbled.

"Bad ankle, Mark?"

"Bad legs."

"What happened?"

"Thinking."

Bill Baeren and I weren't on intimate terms in person. A year, year-and-a-half before, when I'd answered his classified ad in S.U.'s campus weekly paper, we'd met for a standard job interview. Neither here nor there, he'd turned me over to his departing 'night assistant' (that is, a 'peeper' like me) for an on-the-job breaking-in and evaluation. Baeren and I had met an average of once-a-month since then, sometimes on errands, usually by accident.

Bill Baeren prefers to keep his business affairs on his own shoulders and his public relations image to be that of the "individual", "a man working alone for the truth." What that means is simple enough: client-type people are nervous enough about divorce detectives, they want privacy, and, even though anyone with half a brain can figure out that Baeren can't do it alone, clients prefer to confess their suspicions to the man in charge, not his staff. Especially when Bill's specialty is Adultery - the Big A that kills love, crushes egos and can even reduce Alimony (the other Big A) to the size of a pea - or bring sparkling diamonds back into the eyes of the mortally heartbroken Loyal Wife & Mother of Your Children. My divorce, putting aside the ten thousand Fuck You's that preceded the paperwork, was an amiable ramble through the courthouse gardens compared to the critical-mass imploding acrimony of a cuckolded spouse.

The result of this business model was that I was on close terms with an ever-changing line-up of secretary-messengers, had grown to love the paycheck-bringing Postal Service, and never developed any sort of rapport with the person of Bill Baeren.

Which did not stop us from becoming telephone intimates.

Some people can't stand talking on the telephone, others can't live without one. I always picture Bill Baeren's image of professional success as being possessor of an office devoid of personnel, directing a law firm completely by telephone communication. Only as a disembodied voice, I believe, could he allow himself the easy give-and-take of conversation, the joke, the sharp command. I'm not all that perceptive to have observed and concluded this on my own: I learned it from one of his secretaries (I think it was Judy, the March-June '77 lady). While I was talking to her one day about how easy it was to speak with Baeren over the phone, Judy admitted to an uneasiness in the non-electronics office relationship she had with him. I wondered how Bill talked with his family.

I had plenty of time to mull over these impressions because it wasn't until we'd sat down at a small round table and separated ourselves by two beers apiece that Bill Baeren stopped talking about my legs and leg cramps in general. I guess it was the steady rumble of the bowling alley that put him a little back at ease, vibrating through the floor, distancing us.

We didn't talk much during the first, fast, beer. I began to feel warm and beer-sleepy mid-way through the second. Eric Clapton started singing "I Shot The Sheriff" on the jukebox. It wasn't as good as the Bob Marley original but, hell, we were all honkies in here and Syracuse ain't Jamaica, so the beer made it sound better than it deserved. Besides, Clapton can play the guitar like a dream come true, so who listens to his voice anyway? Somewhere over the rainbow.

"Why did you call the police?" I asked, a dopey smile spoiling the frown I had carefully arranged across my brow.

"Mark, about that, I don't think you-"

"Why did you call the police, Bill?"

"I didn't."

I stood up. I looked across at Baeren, put on my best 'ol buddy grin, and said in a loud clear voice, "Bill Baeren, you old bastard, how's business?" I sat down.

Nobody noticed but Baeren - and you'd have thought I'd stood up in church and danced the fandango up the center aisle the way he started, stuttered, and looked around like a sinner damned by a small-town God.

"They called me up! I don't know how they knew. Maybe they saw your name as witness in divorce records somewhere. Maybe they followed you, tapped your phone. You gave them your address, didn't you?"

"Yeah."

"What-a-you expect then?! You're not hiding, it's in the open, they check out witnesses. They called me. I had to tell them the truth."

"About moonlighting? That I was moonlighting, Bill?"

Pause. Beer.

Pause. Talk. Me.

I stood up again.

"Hello, Bill, you old son-of-a-bitch! How's..." He grabbed hard and pulled me down.

"Mark! You're just a stupid peeper. They'll yell at you, OK, but they won't hurt you. I'm supposed to know better. I'm supposed to give them all I've got."

"Then why didn't you?"

The small man looked hurt at that, defeated.

"Hell, Mark, you'd already told me you were going to do it once, tell them everything. You practically threatened me with it. Then you didn't. You yelled at me last night," Bill whined like he had when I'd shown up at his house. "I didn't know what you were going to do." He swallowed. Air, not beer. "What did you say, anyway?"

It was my turn to talk. I swallowed. Beer, not air. I'd give him something, then ask.

"I said enough to keep you out of it if you want."

I swallowed again. Air, not beer - the glass was empty.

"You want out of it, Bill?"

It was the wrong approach. Bill Baeren wanted an escape and he grabbed at it. And I'd let him. "Let"? I had offered it to him!

Baeren spent the next five minutes elaborating on the theme of Responsibilities - he to family, police to society, he to business, me to him, he to him - all of which could have been summed up by a simple "Yes, I want out" at the start.

But I had my answer: Bill Baeren would stand by his statement to Anderson that he knew nothing beyond the fact that I must have been moonlighting that night. I knew where to go from there.

"So I'm out of it, right, Mark?"

"You're out of it, Bill - at least as far as the police are concerned."

It took Baeren a second to get over his relief and realize what I'd just said. Then I said more.

"I want Davis Malloy's file, Bill."

Baeren looked at me like I was swallowing acid and forcing him to watch me do it. I helped him out.

"You're safe, Bill, but I want his file. Give me the Malloy file."

"It's gone, Mark."

"Gone! What do you mean go-"

Visions of grand conspiracies danced in my head. Baeren cut them off with a quick:

"I threw them out yesterday, as soon as you told me she was killed."

"*Merde.*"

My legs were beginning to excruciate. The beer wasn't helping: I hated beer. The taste now was Early

Soapsuds. I looked at the label: Utica Club - I should have known.

I swallowed the bile and reached for my pen and a table napkin simultaneously. Later I would be grateful for the haphazardness of my record-keeping, at the moment I was cursing the flimsy paper that would tear on every third word I wrote.

"Tell me what you remember, Bill."

I lucked out there: I still had the photograph of Anne Malloy that Davis Malloy had given Baeren - and our descriptions of Davis Malloy matched; I had the drinking information and I had the home address (discovered by both of us, I learned, from the telephone book and not from Mr. Davis Malloy). I also knew about Anne Malloy's supposed 'visit' to a cousin on Sunday night that Davis Malloy said he suspected was a visit to 210 Salina Street: the reason we'd been hired.

But I also had some questions that Bill Baeren hadn't thought about.

"How'd you get the drinking info?"

"Same place as I'd gotten his address, the telephone book. Two listings." I should have known, the telephone: a natural for Bill Baeren.

"I checked his office number," he continued, "E.S.C.O., then phoned some friends who work there. No trouble. He's pretty talented with the chemicals and he drinks large and well. I just asked casually, for something to have available, in case of bills and…"

"and… yeah. E.S.C.O.?"

"E.S.C.O., yeah, that's where he works. E.S.C.O. The Chemical company. Out on Lake Onondaga. You remember, Mark: Salt? Chemicals? The dozen or so industries that employ half of Syracuse? E.S.C.O.'s one of them."

I had a question about E.S.C.O. percolating in the back of my head, but it wasn't taking shape yet, so I shifted to Davis Malloy's home life.

"You kept the questioning casual," I asked, "but did you get any more personal? I mean, did they tell you anything more about him, friends from work kind of things?"

"I think he has a home out in Belle-Fredonia, or land maybe. I heard something about land."

"Yeah. I heard about that, too," but I wrote down the 'Belle-Fredonia' to remember this time what I had forgotten about since hearing it before.

"And his kid's sick."

"And - ?"

"And-"

Baeren's forehead drew up in a knot of lines that I guess indicated a memory engaged, then he sighed, "- and I didn't do a lot of background because he paid the deposit up-front, in cash, and it didn't seem out of the routine."

I was finished. Baeren didn't have any more that I could use.

"His kid's dead," I said. "Died Saturday morning."

Baeren turned a sort of sickly color. Or maybe it was just the effect of standing up under a fluorescent light. Bill's eyes glowed brighter than the fluorescents as he exclaimed:

"He didn't come to me till Saturday afternoon!"

But I already knew that.

chapter

fifteen

The trip to 210 Salina Street took me longer than I'd planned on. Icy roads from an early frost nearly made me plow my fender into a Corvette's tail and my teeth through the steering wheel. I detoured twice: once to avoid a hill I didn't feel like sliding down, once to my apartment for a warmer coat. With the slower speed and side trips I didn't arrive at my Sunday night waiting spot across the street from 210 Salina until after eleven. This time I was just parking. I planned to be inside 210. The superintendent wasn't too thrilled about the time of night nor my presence when he opened his door. I didn't feel terribly guilty, though, since he was wide awake and sarcastic enough for the both of us.

"Want to come into my kitchen, friend? I have another telephone you can 'use'."

I deserved it, but I wasn't caring too much any more.

"You didn't tell me about Malloy renting the apartment," I said.

"You didn't ask."

He stepped behind the door. I stuck a textbook in the way before he could slam it fully shut.

"I asked," I said. "You want me to start shoving?"

He opened the door quickly, stepped past me, then closed the door behind his back and in my face. We stood leaning on walls in the basement hallway.

"My wife's asleep. I don't need your noise."

"And I don't need finding things out from the police. I asked you this morning 'what did you know?' You were supposed to tell me straight then."

"You're not from the police?"

"You knew it."

"Well, then, maybe I'd better call the police now."

"Do."

He didn't move.

"Who did you think I was?"

"You said you worked on the Syracuse Star."

I snorted. "I'll swear to it again if I have to. Who did you think I was?"

He looked at me a long time. For a man who

didn't want to let on about certain things, he was taking a lot of chances - for the second time that day I could tell he was putting some sort of trust in me.

"I don't know," he said. "I don't know who I was thinking you were. But," his hand was examining a loose screw on the light switch, "I was expecting it."

He turned the lights out. I watched him do it. He simply pushed the button and the world blacked out. Then he rammed his head into my stomach.

I wasn't thinking when he did it, and one second later I was on the floor gagging.

Only, he was on the floor beside me, hurting bad.

He was on the floor beside me because the first thing I did when the air was knocked out of my stomach was to bring my knees up and my fists down. I wasn't defending myself, I was contracting in pain - fists right onto the back of his head and knees to his face.

But that was his problem. Me, I didn't even care about how successfully I'd downed my assailant. I was trying to uncollapse my lungs, to breathe and not throw up at the same time. My throat felt like there was a fist inside it, gagging and pulling at the muscles of my chest and stomach. I lay rolling on the concrete floor fighting the blackness of unconsciousness that threatened to envelope the blackness of the hallway. After a minute, I won. I began to breathe regular breaths and my eyes started adjusting to the darkness, seeing the hallway's shapes and corners in a monochrome of Impressionist imagery.

Slowly I became aware of another figure lying near me. The superintendent was softly groaning and struggling to come out of the unconsciousness he had not been able to escape.

I groped my way to a standing position, then felt along the wall till I found the light switch. A moment later, I looked my adversary over.

His mouth and teeth were covered with blood in the gummy profusion that told of a broken nose. Occasionally an air bubble of blood blew out of his nose, followed by a fresh rush of red. I looked at my pants. Despite a sharp pain in the knees that told of the encounter with his head, there was no blood on them - he must have pitched face-first onto the concrete and broken his nose there - not that it mattered much in terms of who was responsible. I was glad that my pants were clean.

I pushed the elevator button. By the time the elevator arrived the super was on his knees, totally free of hand support. I helped him to his feet about a minute before he wanted it, then I pushed him into the elevator which he didn't want at all. I left my book on the floor. I didn't remember it until the next day. I couldn't have sold it back to the university bookstore anyway: the binding was broken from being jammed in a door.

The major bleeding from his nose had started when the super hit the floor. By the time we reached the sixth floor, time and my handkerchief stopped the dripping enough that we could walk the halls without leaving a trail. I left it to him to worry about cleaning the elevator.

I walked the superintendent ahead of me, towards 6E, the apartment with the broken window. Funny about that window. When I was talking with Anderson I had an answer to the Suicide v. Murder question, an answer that he already knew: no woman committed suicide by throwing herself through a closed window. When we reached Apartment 6E I was relieved when the super pulled out his master key: what little bravado I had left was relying on momentum now - it would not have survived a trip back down to fetch keys.

The apartment had never been 'empty'. The living room was dominated by a long conference table, while the bedroom, though far from 'lived in,' was outfitted for sleeping - complete with bed, chairs, linen and a dresser drawers. Reminiscent of a permanent arrangement, not a convenient shack-up for Ray St. Johns. Everything was a little too nice for an "empty" apartment.

The superintendent, speaking through the blood-soaked handkerchief, was quick to point out what the police must have already noticed.

"The management rents this out for conferences, sometimes two, three times a month. For people who want small conferences, not seventy-five people places like in hotels." He sat down at one of the dozen straight chairs around the conference table, tilting his head back to staunch the blood flow.

I mulled it over, the situation. Feasible. Hotels charged one hundred to two hundred dollars for their conference rooms per afternoon. For large groups. But there were lots of small businesses in Syracuse, or any city for that matter, businesses that needed a conference space bigger than an office, more intimate than a restaurant, and just about in their price line with an eight to twelve person conference space for...

"How much they ask?"

"Fifty. Seventy-five."

Fine. And the apartment rent would be made without any real wear-and-tear. As for the key, more people than Ray St. Johns could be walking around Syracuse with copies for this place. But I only cared about one.

"When did Davis Malloy rent this apartment?"

The superintendent looked through eyes swollen by more than a broken nose. There was fear there.

Fear and . . . Call it an intense dislike.

He answered grudgingly: "Mid-September. He rented it in September, that what I remember from looking it up for the police. I'd need my calendar to tell you the exact date."

"Don't bother. 'He ever rent it before?"

"Once, maybe a year ago, maybe more. Maybe once before that even. I'd need to check."

"Who are the others that rent this apartment?"

A police question, he gave it a police answer.

"Small businesses. Individuals. They need-"

"What small businesses? Which individuals?"

"I can't remember names."

"Try." I glanced around: telephone, kitchen, intercom, television.

"Well, Malloy. He was renting for E.S.C.O. Uh, sometimes E.S.T.O. has a man call for a small conference, I don't remember names. I really don't."

"E.S.C.O., E.S.T.O., can't give me the rest, though?"

He didn't like my poetry. I did, but I was embarrassed for saying it. He took my embarrassment for a cue and stood up, starting to leave.

"Not very small companies, are they?" I said it just to sound intelligent.

But he answered -

"I don't pay attention."

- answered a little too fast and a little too insistent, repeating:

"I don't pay attention."

I tried to think of more things to ask, not to lose the opportunity. Only the police questions came to me: 'Was the door open when the police arrived?' 'Where's the fire exit?' 'Who didn't return their key?' They were the wrong questions, questions with answers easy to give. I gave up. I tried only diplomacy.

"Do you do all the wiring?"

He pressed the handkerchief to his face, a face so swollen now that it was a mask that spoke, an expressionless mask. Waiting until we were out in the hall, the superintendent closed the apartment door, locked it, then faced me. The eyes of the mask looked into my eyes again, looking for something they could trust.

"Yeah," he said and left me standing there.

He said it like a confession of murder.

chapter

sixteen

I didn't leave my bed the next day until my
bladder nearly burst.

Even then, it was a crawl to the bathroom
followed by a crawl back into bed. I wasn't tired - I was
stiff. Not just in the legs, maybe I could have moved
around on that one, but the nose-busted super had
hurt more than just my stomach when he butted me
down: my kidneys must have shared the wealth to
some extent as well, for I felt the rabbit-punch of their
malfunctioning. A dry spit into a wad of toilet paper
revealed flecks of blood. Christ! Something inside
my precious me had been bleeding and my kidneys
were working overtime fighting the infection that was
threatening to settle in.

Lying in my bed, I fumbled through the side
pockets of a flight bag gathering dust underneath it, till
I came up with a handful of small bottles. One of them
contained what I sought: a year-old prescription for

penicillin. I swallowed two tablets dry, then realized they would do me little good hanging around in my esophagus and crawled into the bathroom for a cup of water. Cold water. My ribs ached from the effort of breathing. I stared hollowly from my perch on the sink, out into the living room and down the three miles to my bed. I gave up contemplation of further exertion and sank down onto the floor, against the cold enamel of the bathtub, groaning.

A minute later, a voice: "OK. Get up."

Another voice answered: "Why?"

First voice, stupidly: "I don' know. I mean, I don' know. You've got to do it, I guess."

"Do what?"

I had me stumped. What do I do now? A sly grin stole across my face as my eyes slid to the left, followed by a stiffly swiveling head. Hot water. I eased myself a foot off the floor and slid over the side into the bathtub. Seconds later acres of fog covered Syracuse mysteriously, a dark warm mist unknown outside of Guatemala, a rain forest humidity which had its fiery origins in the stream of water scalding (albeit with masochistic pleasure) my feet, loins, almost corpse.

I made a mental note to remember my simple, gentle, plumber-superintendent with a handsome tip at Christmastime. I was proud to know a man who had no interest in electricity.

* * * * * * * *

Six hours later, I was a half-comfortable cripple eating fried eggs and rice, seated before a small black television set. It was nine o'clock at night and I was watching a movie I had wanted to see for a long time. Later that Wednesday night, Ray St. Johns' world would fall down around his head. I went to bed when the movie was over.

I slept pretty well.

chapter

seventeen

Thursday took a long time to get through. I didn't try to think about the murder, I didn't want to, but the thoughts came anyway. I had never seen anyone die before: a woman flying through a window was a spectacular initiation.

"God," I pleaded, trying to bargain with my thoughts, "let me rest for two or three days. I'll find out. I will." I knew I had to. But the thoughts came as they pleased, on the second day of recuperation, despite my efforts.

I sat in my chair, kidneys throbbing, and thought of Anne Malloy.

Who wasn't Anne Malloy.

I thought of a red-haired woman with a pleasing face (a little tense about the mouth), freckled and looking at a camera. She wore the black armband of mourning...

Did she know Davis Malloy?

Of course she did: he sent her, she knew his kid.

He hired a divorce detective to catch her committing adultery. -

They had no legal connection.

Or none that I knew of.

I looked at her photograph: a Polaroid starting to curl. The black armband the woman wore told me that she knew Davis Malloy on more than a one-time, business-only basis. The armband gave the photo a date and time: it had been taken Saturday afternoon, after the death of Malloy's son. It had been taken hurriedly, with an instant-developing Polaroid camera, just before Davis Malloy paid a visit to Bill Baeren. But there was one thing the armband didn't tell me, the photo didn't tell me -

Who was she?

She didn't deserve to die the way she did, whatever her name.

I would call her Anne Malloy.

I played Bill Baeren, Master of Phones. Pulling out the Onondaga County directory from under my telephone, I searched for the number of Davis Malloy. He had two numbers under his name: what I knew was his home phone and, by the prefix, what I assumed was a direct dial to his office number.

A workaholic, then, if he needed to put both numbers in. Dialing Malloy's Solvay home listing, I waited. The phone rang ten times. A solid minute. Then I cradled the receiver in my palm, cutting the connection with a forefinger. I started to dial his office telephone, the E.S.C.O. listing -

- when I opted for curiosity instead.

Replacing the receiver in the cradle, I began leafing through the telephone directory. I didn't find 'E.S.C.O.'. I did find the company's full name: Eastern States Chemical Organization.

About four o'clock in the afternoon I started doing exercises, slow and easy, to bring my legs back to life and make the blood flush through my kidneys. I tried watching TV while moving my muscles, but the local news was about another violent crime that I didn't have the spare emotional capacity to think about. Something about a shotgun and a bar. My thoughts were on a woman and a window. When I thought about her my exercises got faster. Angrier. Till I hurt again and forced myself to slow down.

The news repeated itself at 4:30 and the shotgun shooting in the bar took on some more gory details that made me flick the switch and find my bliss inside a half-hour of yoga stretching laid out in front of a blank screen. About five o'clock Detective Lieutenant Anderson showed up. He was carrying my coat.

I answered the door wearing a pair of sweat pants and nothing else. Anderson looked at my chest with its concentric rings of mottled purple and yellow bruise through eyes that did not convey a sense of pleasure at the data they were receiving. They were the doctor eyes again, and I was the symptom. He took the open door for an invitation and walked in.

"I thought I'd bring your coat back, Mr. Cornell, since I had to pay a visit anyway."

He added, "My wife had it cleaned."

"Say 'thank you' for me."

Anderson's eyes surveyed my living quarters. His voice sharpened.

"I had some questions to ask of the superintendent at 210 Salina Street," Anderson said. "His wife told me she hadn't seen him since yesterday."

"No?"

"No. It seems that some honky - Excuse me, my word, not hers - some white man beat up her husband Tuesday night, the day before yesterday. Broke his nose. He went to the hospital emergency ward about one a.m. yesterday morning and she hasn't seen him since."

Anderson didn't look hungry, so I offered: "You want something to eat? It's about my dinner time."

He did.

Grumbling something to myself about the pitfalls of hospitality, I shuffled into the kitchen, Anderson behind me. Wordlessly, he slid into a chair at the kitchen table, my chair, and picked up the nearest of many scattered books lying there, *Crime and Punishment*. Seeing that he was leafing through it, I almost laughed at the irony, when he laid it down and said, "It's better in Russian."

I left our dinner unsliced, ambled painfully into the living room and returned carrying a book filled with Dostoyevski's delicious Cyrillic phrases. Anderson took it haphazardly, then said, "Old alphabet version."

He got liverwurst instead.

It wasn't bad liverwurst. Thick between two slices of white gum, the whole ensemble only stuck to the roof of my mouth when I ate. But the mayonnaise and ketchup I'd slipped in kept my tongue's exercise to a minimum. Anderson appeared to be experiencing the same culinary challenges, but within three minutes we were finished eating and resumed our conversation.

"I was not happy that the superintendent at 210 Salina Street was gone..." he began.

"I know anything the superintendent would feel like telling you."

Anderson nodded. I went on.

"The apartment is used for conferences and, I think, for things illegal."

"What sort of things?"

"I... You know the area: close enough to the poor boys for the people with some disposable income to do some slumming without drawing attention."

"What kind of 'slumming' do business executives do there, Mr. Cornell, with or without 'disposable income'?"

Anderson had caught me in my own easy cynicism: I hadn't clarified the 'illegalities' in my own mind yet. With nothing intelligent to add, I answered with the obvious (also easy) accusation: "Besides, the superintendent's gone. It points to a racket."

Anderson laughed, a short sarcastic slapping sound. I plunged on, "I have more if you want answers."

Anderson cut me short.

"I didn't say I didn't talk to him."

"But... he's gone, isn't he?"

"To Rochester," Anderson began his denouement. "After his wife mentioned his little run-in Tuesday night - by the way, you weren't there, were you? -"

"No."

"I didn't think so. - After talking to her I telephoned his employer on the off chance that a man running away might try to have a little paycheck or something to help him along. It appears that this superintendent, Brandon-"

"'That his name?"

Anderson looked at me a little incredulously.

"I didn't think to ask," I offered lamely.

"Brandon," he repeated for my benefit, using it as salt on an ego wound. "I telephoned his employer and they informed me that 'Mr. Brandon has been transferred to Rochester.'"

Anderson looked at me for a comment. I had one ready:

"Oh."

"Oh."

I expected and deserved a sarcastic remark or raised eyebrow to beat me down for my post-Nixon Era conspiracy theorizing - but instead the detective lieutenant surprised me with a rueful smile that held genuine sympathy. The rueful smile translated into a more considered and deliberate narrative of his investigation:

"When I mentioned the fact that Brandon's wife had not been informed of this fact, about his transfer, the secretary at the E.S.T.O. office was truly surprised.

Mr. Brandon, she explained, had received notice of the transfer two weeks before. A copy of the letter was there in her file."

"But, of course-" I began.

Anderson dramatized his stopping me with a hand in the air and an over-courteous, "*Nyet, spasiba.*"

"Brandon was in Rochester," Anderson said firmly. "He was exactly where they told me he'd be."

Another rueful smile.

"Mr. Brandon, in fact, answered every one of my questions about the apartment."

Anderson stopped talking and let his finger doodle across the Formica-topped kitchen table, drawing invisible designs. His eyes were concentrated on the task, waiting from me to say something. I did.

"You should be happy: him answering all your questions, it closed the doors to a lot of blind alleys you could have gone down."

The finger-doodles continued. Anderson said:

"He even answered questions I hadn't thought of asking -" Anderson looked up from his latest invisible drawing, "- closing a lot of doors Brandon couldn't have known about."

"So you pushed him for better answers and what did he say?" I asked, forgetting that I was on a different side of the equation than Anderson.

Anderson didn't notice my presumption, or he didn't care. He answered as if I deserved his confidence:

"I wasn't investigating Brandon's midnight fight and flight and I couldn't push him to answer over the telephone. As far as Brandon is concerned, he left Syracuse under normal conditions - and couldn't understand what his wife was talking about. He thinks she is probably playing hysterical for the police and - 'Yes,' he admits - there is a woman involved."

"Ties up a lot of loose ends," I shot in. "Want dessert?"

"What is it?"

"Yogurt."

"With raspberries? Blueberries?"

"Lemon."

"No."

"Tell you what," I advised, "why don't you check into the management of 210 Salina Street, the Eastern States Title Operators, and see how their alibis hold up?"

"E.S.T.O. - And find what?" Anderson shot back. "A three-state corporation that represents the norm of the American real estate business, and publishes its affairs in *Fortune* magazine?"

He flashed a pained grimace intended to convey a smile.

"I checked that out. I checked it out enough to know that what E.S.T.O. does is clean, give-or-take a local zoning violation, and that their affairs are an open and closed book. For a police investigation."

He made his point, but I was fascinated by the details. I had never talked to a real, live police detective before. Or any detective other than Bill Baeren, and I don't think Bill is qualified to be considered in the same league. Or profession.

"How open and closed?" I asked.

"Open enough that I can look at anything I want to and talk to anyone I want to. That open. It's a legitimate enterprise."

"So...?"

"Closed enough that a lot of - egos - would be hurt."

Anderson shook his head through some thoughts. "It's true," he said, "we're not talking cover-up from that side. Honest folk can't stand to be investigated. And when they are... And when they have political clout..."

He looked at me for support.

"There's no pressure at all. 'You understand that? But I'd be a fool to look for nothings. And there's nothing." He leafed through Dostoyevski. "Nothing."

"You know more than I do," Anderson added. He wasn't asking.

"Yes."

"Any of it evidence? Hard?"

After a moment, he answered himself:

"Nothing."

I abandoned Anderson, leaving him sitting in the kitchen, and went to the telephone in the living room. A short, five-step journey of a thousand pained muscles. Dialing a certain number in Solvay, the only one I knew, I noticed the dark form of the police detective slide behind me into the armchair facing the window. My chair. He was watching the sunset.

"Hello? Malloy residence." Even through the electronic thinness of the receiver the voice sounded firm, stolid.

Anderson did not take his eyes off the sun. It was a comfortable chair he sat in.

"I'd like to speak with you this evening, Mr. Malloy, about your wife."

A weary voice, sounding justified, answered me. "My wife has been dead for four years, Mister...?"

"Divorce detective. I'm the one Bill Baeren hired to peep on Anne Malloy. I can be right over if it's convenient."

"Nothing is convenient this week. I will expect you."

Unlike myself, Anderson wasn't surprised by my success in getting through to Davis Malloy and setting up a meeting. In fact, he was dozing. I shook him gently awake. "Don't you ever sleep?" I asked.

"I do pretty good between seven a.m. and one in the afternoon."

"Not very convenient when you're on day shift."

"Gives you a home life, though: take it where you can get it."

We watched the sunset. Damn, they have good sunsets in Syracuse. I don't know if anything else is worthwhile living for in Syracuse. I know there's nothing else from my window. Not bad sunrises either, I'm told. I don't know, I can't see them from my window.

"'Want to visit Solvay?" I asked.

"No."

"Coming anyway?"

"Yeah."

We took my car. I charged the mileage to Bill Baeren - I didn't think he'd complain under the circumstances. On the way I asked Anderson, "Are you on duty now or off?"

"I don't know," the police detective next to me said, "I don't…"

The house was empty when we got there. Doors locked, not a light on. A note on the front door told the newsboy to leave the daily paper at a neighbor's. It was dated Tuesday. It was the same note Anderson had seen on his first visit to Solvay. It said that Davis Malloy would leave a note when he returned.

"You heard the conversation," I said.

"Nothing."

* * * * * * * * *

We returned to Syracuse to pick up Anderson's car near my apartment. He came up to the apartment with me, to use my telephone.

Anderson left five minutes later. His investigation would be finished shortly, he said. There was just enough work to do at the present, and just enough chance that it was a suicide, that the case would be handed over to the Missing Persons Bureau to be buried in their files among the runaway kids and the Friday-night fathers. Federal investigators weren't interested: there wasn't enough evidence to justify their presence. State investigators, finding no evidence of drugs, were leaving it all in the city's hands.

Anderson left my apartment carrying a copy of *The Possessed,* in Russian, old alphabet. He and I figured we would get together soon and discuss it.

We'd both read it before, but some things are worth looking at a second time.

chapter

eighteen

If I had sought it out on purpose I could not have found a better antidote to the restlessness I was feeling: a three-hour lecture on Medieval French Verse in Relationship to Chaucer's Poetry.

Whan that Aprill, with his shoures soote

Mais ou sont les neiges d'antan?

Nope, not yesterday. Today

Still too stiff to follow up on any of my thoughts, I had decided to attend Thursday night class. To get there, thanks to one-way streets, I had to drive down Genesee Street and swing up by the S.U. Theatre Department, plopped down about a mile downhill from campus in the middle of the ghetto. I didn't mind the side trip, since "The Salt City Repertory Company - only 279 miles from Broadway!" sometimes boasted some visiting pros who lifted the grad school productions up a notch and I was in the mood for culture. But the marquee was blank so I guessed they were between productions. (No, let's not go down that road of "Why didn't you look it up in a newspaper?")

Across the street from the Theatre Department was Flora's, a black bar that catered mainly to townies but occasionally tolerated the white kids from across the street who wandered in late nights after rehearsals. After the-ah-tuh my thoughts turned to booze, but Flora's was closed. Very closed. Big police barriers covering the entrance and plywood hastily nailed behind a smashed front window. Damn!, Flora's hadn't been closed since the Spring '70 student riots closed down S.U. - and even then the students had been too afraid of the brothers to do any damage to the place. Theatre students rioting - yeah! I was up on the Quad, in my Biz School phase I think, and despite being bummed out by Nixon's National Guard killing the Kent State 4, I was pragmatic enough to realize that the real motivation for most students protesting was extremely bad dorm food and the 50-50 chance that Finals would be cancelled. In both cases the gamble paid off: Finals were cancelled without penalty and the head of Student Food Services was canned for skimming from the budget. Meals for the Fall 1970 semester improved immediately. Flora's was unmolested.

Till now. I remembered something from yesterday's news about a shotgun and a bar and bodies blown apart and remembered that I still didn't have the extra emotional reserves to think about more than one close-distance tragedy at a time. Forget the *News At Four*, time for *Chaucer At Seven*.

I have never been fond of evening classes, but this night was a gift from heaven. Seated comfortably in the center of a lecture hall (class of sixty, space for three hundred), I eased down into an over-stuffed, alumni-paid-for cinema-style seat (as opposed to the creaky-old, hard-backed wooden auditorium "deskettes" standard in the Hall of Languages building across the Quad), while three fine fellow graduate students (doctoral candidates, actually) droned on for an hour apiece on the various virtues and defects of.....

I woke to the brush of a nylon parka across my forehead -

- and saw the co-ed who had been seated behind me slipping her arm into said parka's sleeve.

I looked around, disoriented: oh, yeah - class was over. The chief honcho professor and his three grad assistants-cum-substitute lectors kept glancing in my direction. Had I been snoring?

I returned their furtive glances with a little stare of my own. No problem: the professor was afraid of me, I was too old for his preconceptions.

Besides, I really did like the course. No matter what I did I'd get at least a 'B' - the prof was afraid to give me anything less - but I would earn an 'A' because I had already written the best term paper he was going to see all year. Better than anything the three pre-docs down there with him could come up with. On Villon and *The Wife's Tale*. We likes a good bawdy, we does. Besides, when you're in your twelfth year of this college stuff, if you can't write a decent paper by then, then maybe you should look out for another profession.

Twelve years. - It suddenly hit me that I had been doodling in college as long as I had been in elementary school, junior and senior high school put together. Jeez, it had seemed to take a lifetime getting through those places! How come the last twelve years didn't seem so long?

I was hungry. I needed food. Real food, not campus crap. I headed for my apartment and a refrigerator that had to have something that didn't need frying.

The room smelled like stale beer. I don't like beer enough to drink it at home, so when I opened the door to my apartment the smell hit me like a wet dog. I didn't have time to worry, however.

Ray St. Johns was pointing a .45 caliber revolver in my face.

chapter

nineteen

I had never stared a pistol in the face before. In the half-light of an apartment lit only by a streetlight standing outside the window and three floors below, the .45 - aimed somewhere at the triangle made by the tip of my nose and eyes - created quite a sensation with my heart: that vital organ was suddenly in my mouth. As I often do in such reflex situations, I uttered a witty "Huh!" in a high-pitched voice, followed a half-second later by a sort of stamp-hop with my whole body, jumping back in surprise a full yard's distance without apparently moving my feet.

That was my first reaction. Shock. Panic. Fear.

My second reaction was annoyance. I shouted at St. Johns:

"What the heck are you doing aiming a BB gun at my face!?"

I switched on the lights and slammed the door shut. There it was, in full light: a BB gun facsimile of a .45 caliber revolver, held in the hand of the Ray St. Johns facsimile of a desperate gunman. Ignoring my words, he waved the gun in front of him like it could mincemeat my head.

"Don't move, brotheh, I mean business."

"It's a BB gun, for Christ's sake! What you gonna do, shoot out my eyes?"

"I shoot, we find out."

It wasn't even a CO_2 BB gun, something with an ounce of power, just a hand-pump kid's jobbie. I used to have a BB gun like that when I was ten, so I knew -

"The BBs are gonna bounce off my coat, St. Johns."

He thought about that a moment - not long enough to really think, but at least some indication that he was starting to hear me. Then he waved the gun again and started to repeat:

"I shoot -"

"- we find out. Yeah, I got it." My annoyance was sliding into embarrassment that Ray St. Johns actually made me look like a pro. He was scared, though, and I appreciated that. I stepped into my apartment to help him make the next step easier.

But Ray St. Johns was not quite ready to calm down. He moved around me, gun extended, till he was between me and the door. Then he slipped the chain lock on. All the while, St. Johns maintained a running conversation with himself, describing himself as a "danger-man": "I am bad for you. You see me and you see a badthing", et cetera. I wondered if he had it on a typewritten card somewhere.

I did not move.

I didn't think his shaking hand could hit any target on purpose, but I like my face without accidental BB blackheads. And I like my eyes. So I waited for St. Johns to calm himself down and tell me what to do next. Instead of becoming calmer, though, I could tell (even without benefit of the Psych 408 class) that Ray St. Johns was talking himself in circles of escalating nervousness. It would have to be my move.

Obeying a command he didn't make but couldn't object to, I raised my hands over my head. That made him feel good. One of the hands held a textbook. The *Annotated Chaucer*. Hardcover. It was heavy. When St. Johns wound his way back around to standing in front of me, I threw the book at his head.

For a skinny guy he was strong - after he fainted from the blow I had to struggle to pry loose the gun from his grip. When most people faint their muscles relax, but St. Johns held on like his hand was paralyzed. As I was wriggling the gun loose, I noticed the dried blood spattered across his clothes. As I was wriggling the gun loose, he began to revive. As St. Johns began to revive, I squatted next to him and pointed the BB gun at his right eye.

"You smell like stale beer," I said, which meant nothing beyond the fact that he really stank up the place and I was too upset to say anything intelligent. I wanted to scare him, though, make him feel the same jerky feeling in his bowels that he had just put me through.

I squatted there for a minute, feeling powerful, until I realized that I couldn't shoot his eye out if my life depended on it. Maybe it did. I stood up, threw the gun onto the armchair and began removing my coat.

St. Johns didn't get off the floor. Instead, he curled up, shivering. He wanted to cry, you could tell that from the way his throat muscles kept convulsing. I helped him into the chair, gave him his toy gun, and covered him with my coat. He still shivered, still wanted to cry, but he looked up at me with an easy grin. I liked him. (Which is probably how Satan made friends with Adam and Eve: an easy smile and all was fine.)

"You gonna make it right?" he asked.

"Yeah."

He was calming down now. I was calming down now. We could start talking calmly and make sense.

Or calmly make no sense, which is how the conversation took off from there:

"Why you tell him, brotheh? I didn' know her."

"Know who? Tell who?"

St. Johns' easy smile faded. "You tell me. You know her name. You the one that told me."

"Anne Malloy?"

"You the one that told me."

I threw out the only name that I knew connected with Ray St. Johns: "Brandon? He was the building super."

"Brandon knows shit."

"He's split town."

St. Johns thought about that a moment - really thought this time - then spoke to himself with me listening in:

"Brandon knows shit. He told me a white dude was comin'. Too late he told me. He said the honky was comin' to see the man who was with that little girl..." St. Johns looked up and brought me into his conversation: "You told her man, didn't you? That's who you told."

"Davis Malloy?" I was surprised that St. Johns would bring him up. St. Johns didn't respond to the name, though, so I repeated it: "Davis Malloy."

"If that's his name."

"I didn't tell Davis Malloy anything."

"Shit, you didn't! He her man, yeah? -"

As much as I knew, Davis Malloy was something to Anne Malloy. I nodded a vague "Yes."

Ray St. Johns said intensely, like a man in pain: "He's goin' to kill me."

Nobly grieving Davis Malloy out to kill Ray St. Johns? Some ideas are absurd even without the benefit of course credit in French Philosophy and the Dada/Surrealist Movement. Forgetting Rule #1 of Detective School - let the witness talk - I answered St. Johns without thinking:

"I don't think so."

"He fuckin' well is! What you think I'm doin' here, brotheh? What you think I'm doin'? You tell her man I was gone before she was killed! You tell him!"

St. Johns started waving the gun. And he stayed sitting in the armchair, my coat still draped over him. It looked like he had a rabbit hopping on his lap.

"Tell him I'll fight back now!" St. Johns shouted in my face. "Tell him I'll blow his head off!"

"Not with a BB gun," I said.

The jumping rabbit died.

"Not with no BB gun," St. Johns said quietly,

deflated. He started sobbing, "Not with no real forty-five, either. Not 'gainst no shotgun." He was staring at his lap, crying and talking only for himself. "Not 'gainst no shotgun."

I left him there, crying -

- and went into the kitchen, a reflex action.

I opened the refrigerator and stared at the food. I wasn't hungry anymore. I hadn't been hungry at all, I guess, not since seeing a .45 in my face, however fake, had put squiggles in my intestines, but suddenly the image taking shape in my thoughts made me nauseous at the sight of food. I drank a glass of cold water and hurried back to the living room with a refill.

St. Johns was no longer crying. He was staring out my window. He turned to me with his easy grin, drank my proffered water and tossed off my coat.

"I could have shot out your eye, you know that."

I was staring at his own, blood-spattered, coat. I think I nodded 'Yes'. He held up the BB pistol.

"I got this to practice with, for the Reserves. I'm a Marksman."

I was glad he hadn't told me before.

"What happened with Brandon?" I asked. "He's not superintendent of the apartment building anymore: they moved him out to Rochester. Why?"

"Don't know and don't care."

"I do."

St. Johns looked hurt. "Don't you want to know what happened to me?"

I gave him the answer he wanted. "Sure."

Ray St. Johns sniffed the air. "Had a beer," he laughed. "Had a beer!"

I sniffed, too. "You don't say."

"'Didn't finish it, though."

"I can live without beer," I said, voicing the distaste it had earned from me the past few days.

St. Johns looked at me like I had uttered a blasphemy. "I like beer... You never in the Army, right?"

"No."

"I like beer."

He was seeing a beer that he liked, from a place that he hadn't, then he turned to me and asked: "You know Flora's?"

"Black bar?"

"Across the street from that damn university's theater." He said it delicately: The-a-tuh. "Why'd they go and put it down in the middle of the Project?"

I waited. So did he. I guessed he wanted an answer. "Why'd they go'n put a student the-a-tuh down'n The Project?" he asked again.

"Probably 'cause the university owns The Project," I offered.

"Must," he agreed. "White ivory tower owns black ghetto, sounds logical. They rippin' it down and makin' a mental hospital there, you know."

"Flora's?" I prompted. He nodded vaguely; I took it for a "Yes".

"Lot's a white folks come in and outta that the-a-tuh every night. Nobody come across the street into Flora's anymore. They walk by, on their side. Last night, some white man come across the street and try to blast Ray's head off."

He said it calmly, a far away memory. It was now. It was about to become a part of the Ray St. Johns 'legend'. St. Johns began warming up to the story, no longer afraid that someone was trying to kill him, but that he was making an impression on me by telling it.

"White man comes to the door, kicks it open.

"'St. Johns!' he yells and pulls out this shotgun.

"But he not knowin' that I been in 'Nam: I seen fragging grenades. I jumped before.

"I jumped then, too!, right over that bar!

"I don't know if he really knew who I was, but he blasted poor Flora, who was still standin' there ready to take my money. Blasted the beer right out of her hand, the hand right off a her arm. Right off her arm...

'Nam-time again - *Neebu hatchi* - No way, baby - no way: Raybo, he not goin' down, girl, keep your head low, grab me a beer, protect my bulls, c'mon li'l Suki we can make it through the night..."

He was lost two days and five years back and I needed him now.

"Ray," I said between his croons to li'l Suki, "what did you see at Flora's? Who was it?"

His eyes fast-flicked my question away as unworthy.

"Me? I'm right behind that bar, down low."

"What did you hear? Did he say anything?"

"All I hear is noise, all kind a noise. And he is gone."

"What did you tell the police?"

St. Johns looked at me like it was the most natural thing in the world that he was explaining.

"I didn't stay for the police," he said.

"Why not?"

"I'm the only one heard what that white man said. What he really said. All the others had a sort of... 'imagination' about what happened. Even before I got up from the floor, I hear one nigger tellin' how it was the Mafia come to shake down Flora, callin' her 'Small Change' and bein' off his aim. Another nigger

is answerin' him that it's some white Baptist preach-
er cryin' 'Jesus Saves!' and makin' a example a poor
Flora. I knew the police weren't gonna listen to me...

"And they weren't gonna protec' me, either.
That's why I come to you. You tell him now that it
wasn't Ray. You tell her man that: it wasn't Ray killed
her."

"Why should I?"

"'Cause you know better, brotheh!"

"No - I don't," I answered, slowly, trying to think
of a way to understand this new development, to coax
more information from St. Johns. I wanted to say this
one right, "You gave me nothing Tuesday," I said as
harshly as I could command my voice to work. "All
I've got is a card that Anne Malloy had in her hand. If
I just read the card it tells me that 'lover-man' - you -
probably killed her."

"I was gone!"

"Prove it."

"How?"

"Your card."

St. Johns was it: the only one who could tell me
what Anne Malloy was doing there. Maybe Davis Malloy could, too, but he was for tomorrow. I was going to
use Ray St. Johns while I had him.

"How did she get your card?" I demanded. "You were with her, I know that," I lied. "How long were you with her and what did you say?"

St. Johns leaned forward to take me into his confidence.

"I hid out last night," he said. "I ran home, got my gun, and hid out. All last night and all today."

His concentration vied with mine for lack of continuity: a new thought jostled its way into my words.

"Excuse me, I'll be right back."

I walked over to the front door, unchained it, opened it, and went to the door across the hall. After three swift knocks, the door was answered by the fifty year-old woman of the house, Mrs. Oscars. Mrs. Oscars loves me, thinks I am a handsome boy, can do no wrong and wouldn't I like to visit her more often? I often want to, but know I couldn't handle the guilt feelings, so I make sure my visits are always during non-office hours, when the spouse is at home - Mr. Oscars and I get along fine, too. With such a deep relationship going among us, it was no problem to borrow an evening paper and check out St. Johns' story.

It was more like he said than he said it: the newspaper listed four versions of the incident, each differing in details ranging in scope from the number of gunmen involved to quotations from a five-minute "speech" the killer had delivered before completing his task. Still, the essential facts paralleled St. Johns' account. Besides, he was afraid for his life. I was sure that he'd remember the details for a long time.

I returned the newspaper, promised an afternoon tête-à-tête with Mrs. Oscars, and turned back to my apartment.

The door was closed. Locked. After a minute's pounding, however, St. Johns let me in.

"Don't tell me why," I said, as he chained the door behind me.

"I was already there, the apartment, that night," St. Johns began, after settling himself on the edge of the window sill (I had my chair back). "You heard about Es-telle? 'Time you over at my place, remember? Well, they been other women before Es-telle. I got a good rapport with womens. One there that night."

"Sunday night?"

He counted back the days in his head. "Yeah, Sunday," he agreed uncertainly, then smiled with a more definite clarity. "Nice woman, yeah, Sunday night choc'lit delight."

"You got a name for me?"

"No last names. Or addresses. Only telephone numbers and first names. Easier on my 'conscience'."

"You've got one of those when it comes to women?"

Easy grin. Profile. Full face.

"Well, this little girl, 'Anne' you called her, she comes unlockin' the door and walking in on me just five minutes after I sended my woman home. I was in the bathroom taking a shower." He started picking at the flecks of dried blood on his coat sleeve.

"What did she say when she found you inside the apartment?"

"Nothing. She knew I was in there. Couldn't not know: the bathroom's just off the hall you come in. And she don't say nothing. She waits. Like she expects me to be there.

"Anyway, when I hear the front door open and close I figure it's Brandon comin' to get the apartment key back from me - 'Oh, shit!' I think, 'snagged.' - so I go a little slower, to give him time to be cool about it, and get myself ready to put out some effort at being friendly with him. I'll say this: that little girl saw one friendly nigger come out of that bathroom.

"She small, you know. Small and kinda good to look at, not old, either. I like red hair... She had a pretty mouth, too, I mean 'smile', I didn't get to try out her mouth. She wore-"

"I know what she looked like," I cut in. "I saw her die."

St. Johns darted his eyes at me, insulted, and turned on my remark.

"Saw her die, huh?" His voice rose. "Then you don't really know what she look like alive, do you? What'd her smile look like when you saw her, huh?"

I couldn't honestly answer, so I kept my mouth shut. St. Johns quieted down with that out of the way. "She looked at me like I was important, so I gave her my card. That's when she smiled... Only polite, though, like when you smilin' at a Reg'lar Army lieutenant's joke that wasn't too funny.

"Then she said, 'There's a detective.'"

I jumped inside. "A what?"

"She said, 'There's a detective.' That's all she said, at least to me, 'cause I don't stay around to meet any detectives. I figured that fuckin' Brandon had something goin' on there in that place and I wanted to be out."

"You think Brandon had something illegal running?"

"Yeah! Me! Shit, that Brandon's a electricity man - he don't run businesses - but he was mad at me the last time I was there and probably wanted my tail... At least that's what I thought."

"What did Brandon say to you the last time he talked to you?"

St. Johns looked at me blankly.

"Tuesday?"

Blanker still.

"Tuesday morning - before I came to your place: he tried to call you..."

A thought filled-in the blank expression. "Oh, yeah..."

The thought fleshed itself out: "Not much. Didn't tell me much. He got through after you been and gone, so it was a little late for warnin' words, and I sorta figured you was the helpful-to-Ray kind, which sorta pissed him. But he told me trouble was probably comin', I told him it had, thinking of Es-telle and some. We were on dif'rent vibes, you see - till he asked me if I knew any 'Anne Malloys' and I said I'd heard the name."

I must have looked surprised.

"Well I had," St. Johns said. Staring out the window he easy-grinned his punchline:

"You told me the name."

chapter

twenty

The skinny black man in the Genghis Khan-moustache and bloodstained overcoat looked back at me again. "And now you gonna tell that little girl's man that Ray St. Johns didn't do anything to her."

He walked over to the telephone, picked up the receiver and handed it to me, saying, "I'll even dial the number for you. What is it?"

I pointed out Davis Malloy's Solvay number on a scrap of notepaper next to the phone, and we listened to the faint ringing sound together as I held the receiver out for both of us to hear. No answer. I hadn't expected there to be. St. Johns hadn't expected to be still worrying.

I made him worry even more. It didn't make me feel good doing it.

"I don't know Davis Malloy," I said. "I saw him

once, talked to him on the phone today, and he's disappeared since." Then I said what St. Johns was thinking, "And he's probably after you."

I don't know why I said that - half of what I knew specifically pointed out that Davis Malloy wasn't even related to "Anne Malloy."

But I kept remembering the other half of what I knew about Davis Malloy - and worried for Ray St. Johns: the "justified" voice, the look in his face, the unpretentious way he could buy a round of drinks, sharing his grief without trying to impress others with his pain. This version of Davis Malloy might easily be imagined seeking vengeance on the only man linked to the death of "his woman." Private vengeance. And the only man with a direct link to the last moments in the life of Anne Malloy was Ray St. Johns, lover-man.

And me.

And the person who pushed her out the window.

No, I didn't think it was Ray St. Johns. Not this lover-man who used .45 caliber BB guns to protect his life. And, despite it being a "thought" that had to be considered just to throw it aside, I didn't think Davis Malloy had the slightest idea of lover-man's existence.

But somebody was trying to kill Ray St. Johns and the working proposition started with Davis Malloy in Ray St. Johns' mind.

He started playing with the safety catch of his BB gun, clicking it in and out of lock. "That little girl's man thinks I'm dead. I'm safe I just stay outta sight."

No way not to burst the bubble of illusion.

"Sorry, Ray: if he reads the newspapers, your name's not there."

"Maybe he don't-"

"He reads newspapers."

"Damn!"

"You wanted it there?"

At the thought of his name in the Obit column, St. Johns started moving around the room. Short, jerky steps. "What you tell him for?" he accused, waving the BB gun again.

"I didn't. Maybe Brandon did."

"He's my friend."

"He told me... First."

I was growing tired now of St. Johns. We were going in circles together and he was getting boring. Maybe because he kept asking the same questions I'd been asking myself for the past week. I was tired of those questions.

I didn't even bother to correct St. Johns about Davis Malloy. At least he had a name to be afraid of, instead of jumping at every shadow in the corners.

And I knew that Ray St. Johns should be afraid of every shadow in the corners, but I wasn't going to take away his hopes.

For whatever reason, though, anyone connected with Anne Malloy's death was staying away from me - maybe because of the police connection - and that led me to propose:

"I'll take you home."

St. Johns looked at me with an expression of betrayal. "I'm not going back for no shotgun to find me, I-"

"I'll take you home - then we come back here," I cut him off. "You need to get some other clothes. I don't like the smell of stale beer and you'll never get rid of all the blood without going to a cleaner. You can sleep here after."

The full-length version of my idea agreed with St. Johns. Within a minute we were headed down to the street and my car. I didn't ask Ray where his car was; I figured it was still in need of a battery.

The drive to Forman Street was notable for one reason only: I almost ran into a deer.

The road between my apartment and St. Johns' is mainly residential streets set off by main avenues lined with shopping centers, but a stream runs through the city and into Lake Onondaga, crossing midway between our respective abodes. They called it a river, but more out of nostalgia than in recognition of the Spring flooding season. Occasionally a raccoon wanders downstream into the city and is seen strolling down a street in the moonlight (usually garbage take-out night). Once people claimed they saw a wolf. This time it was a deer.

He was stepping over the pavement slowly when I turned the corner and caught him in my headlights. He froze. I didn't react at first, but kept on driving as I admired the deer's look of wild intelligence. Only at the last moment did I slam on the brakes and avoid ramming into him. Only then did the deer turn and leap, away from the direction of the stream. I saw him head toward a thicket of trees I knew backed into a shopping center parking lot. I drove on, stopped at a pay telephone, and called the police, telling them where I thought he'd run off to. I tried to sound excited and worried, urging them to come out and do something. But the voice answering me sounded bored and annoyed. They'd check it, the voice droned. I drove around to the shopping center. The deer was nowhere in sight. All I saw was a broken display window. On closer inspection there was blood on the glass. But not much.

Lights were on in St. Johns' apartment.

St. Johns eyes were closed, he was dozing, as I woke him with the question: "Do you pay utilities?"

"Yeah," he yawned.

"I think I'll worry," I said.

We saw the open door to his apartment as we came up the stairwell.

Stopping at the top of the landing, we were unable to decide what to do next. St. Johns looked at me as if he expected me to be the expert of us two in crime and criminal ways. I guess it was the beard made me look mature: in a world of clean-shaven teenagers trying to look like John Travolta in *Saturday Night Fever*, it worked with undergrads when I was a grad assistant teaching Freshman English. Especially when I scowled to cover up the fact that I didn't know what to do next. I scowled now and St. Johns looked relieved. It even made me think clearer: glancing at the door, I realized that we were better targets on the landing than we would be at the door - with less to hide behind.

I motioned St. Johns to come close to me and took the BB gun from him for emotional support. We edged up to his open doorway. Stopping just before the door, I grabbed St. Johns by the arm and thrust him through it ahead of me.

The room was empty.

According to St. Johns, with the exception of the lock-broken open door nothing in the room was changed from the way he'd left it. The window was still locked, the stereo was intact, the television in its place - even the sofa-bed, except for the large hole that a shotgun had blasted out, was still at the angle Ray St. Johns had set for comfortable television viewing. The room was empty and we were still alive.

But St. Johns was uninterested in the total decor of his apartment. Ignoring the manner in which his entrance had been made, he stood over the hole in his sofa-bed. A man of many words, he seemed to be stuck on an endless repetition of some phrase I couldn't quite make out and didn't step closer to hear. I left him there to check out the rest of the place.

The walk-in kitchen was intact.

There was a closet with an open door that revealed a mess of clothing, but the chaos looked native to the Ray St. Johns lifestyle.

A quick inspection of the bathroom, intending to relieve the effects of what few nerves I had left, revealed a second door with a broken lock and a second hole perforating the wall two feet above the toilet. About the height of a sitting man's head. Or a standing man's stomach. With a shotgun it didn't matter much which.

Where the hell were the cops and why hadn't anyone called them? Depending on the time of day when the break-in occurred, maybe no one had been around to notice. Depending on the neighbors, maybe no one wanted the police to come too soon before certain "housekeeping" activities had been performed. Depending on the number of women Ray St. Johns had slept with, maybe everyone expected this sooner or later anyway. It wasn't my type of apartment management but, the way things were going, I wouldn't have been surprised if it was owned by E.S.T.O. I left the bathroom unused and went back to St. Johns.

Ray St. Johns' attention was dominated by only one thought - he stood over the remains of his sleeping place and kept repeating, "I'm dead ... I'm dead," in a flat, unemotional tone - like the morphined casualties who watch themselves die with an obsessive, almost casual, objectivity. He wasn't afraid now, because he should have been dead twice already.

I didn't tell him about the bathroom.

I grabbed the first warm clothes that came into my fist out of his closet, took St. Johns' arm with my free hand, and pulled him out of the room. It wasn't worth the effort to try shutting the door: the valuable possessions of Ray St. Johns were on their own.

Five minutes later, idling at a red light, St. Johns finally variated his "I'm dead" chant with an, "I don't want to die." He said it as calmly as he had been saying the earlier mantra. I looked over at him. He was calm. Frozen-with-fear calm.

"'You want to go to the police?" I asked.

"What they do?" he asked. Rhetorically. Not aggressive. Not with despair. Matter-of-fact.

I pulled the car over to a parking space. We were downtown now, 'round midnight, there were plenty available. St. Johns started playing with the safety catch of his BB gun again.

"What the polices gonna do?" he asked again, "Ask me questions? What I got? Nothin'. You got anything for the Man?" He looked at me: "No. Nothin'. So I go to the Man - we go to the Man - we out again in two, three hours. 'We'll look into it,' they'll say. Shit, even they do we out, too! Where you say that little girl's man is?"

"I don't know."

"We out on the street, too." He said it like a death sentence.

Not having anything intelligent to add from my side of the conversation, I pulled the car away from the curb and headed back toward my apartment. Again, for some reason, the Davis Malloy contact was elusive to me, avoiding me - maybe because I was seen with Detective Lieutenant Anderson, maybe because I'd been on the outside of 210 Salina Street talking with a blueshirt when everything happened and clearly knew nothing - making my place safe haven for now. For me. After the violation of Ray St. Johns' apartment and the massacre at Flora's I wasn't sure how far I could push that sanctuary. I had no great desire to link my fate with that of Ray St. Johns.

We passed a movie theater letting out. Dozens of people walking down the midnight streets of Syracuse. More than dozens. Loew's was a big, old-fashioned movie palace, with a popular flick flicking this week. Lots of people, almost exclusively white, paying those ticket prices, filling those sidewalks. When the idea of how to save Ray St. Johns hit me, then, I had to jam on my brakes to avoid slamming into a dirty green Chevy pulling out of the theater parking lot.

"How you like playing crazy black guy?" I asked him.

St. Johns did not react too pleasantly to the phrase I had offered. He didn't answer, either, so I repeated it.

"'You mind staying with the police instead of me? How you like playing crazy black guy?"

"Shut up!"

I gunned the motor and shot down the street, nearly taking two movie-exiters with me. A quarter-mile later, I stomped on the brakes. In the middle of the street. The people spilling out of the theater behind us were gawking in our direction, shaking angry heads. I turned off my lights - I didn't want anybody seeing my license plates.

"What will they do to a crazy black man walking downtown outside of Loew's with a gun in his hand?" I said. I reached across, opened the car door on St. Johns' side, and gave him a solid push. I locked the door behind him.

St. Johns pounded on the door. After three blows, he started kicking. After four kicks, he started grinning. An easy grin.

"Shoot the streetlight and ditch the gun!" I shouted through the closed windows.

St. Johns nodded agreement, then did me one better. As I drove away, he shot out my rear tail light, the right one. I didn't know it at the time.

Five minutes later I was stopped by a police car. I would have gotten a ticket for having only one tail light, but the blueshirt let me off with a warning - he was called downtown to Loew's theater and he didn't have time for me.

"Some crazy black guy's shooting up windows! Get the light fixed!" he shouted from his car.

I hoped St. Johns remembered to get rid of the pistol. It wouldn't do to have the police find out it was only a BB gun. And it wasn't a good idea to get shot for resisting arrest by having it in his hand, either.

* * * * * * * *
* * * * *
*

finding

chapter

twenty-one

I needed Davis Malloy.

Killer or victim, husband or... what? - Davis Malloy could not be kept out of the murder of Anne Malloy. Not now. Not when he was the only person I still hadn't talked to. Beyond cryptic phrases. Not when I didn't have any idea where else to look.

I read in the morning newspaper, bought especially for the occasion, about a black gunman who had been captured in downtown Syracuse early in the morning. The gunman wasn't talking. Bail would not, could not, be set until he could be identified and the man wasn't talking. He would be placed under supervision for evidence of mental incompetence. Ray St. Johns was safe with the police.

For at least a month. Or until I cleared his story, whichever came.

I had slept later than the working man and earlier than my pleasure. Now, when I telephoned

Davis Malloy's number, I tried the Eastern States Chemical Organization listing: E.S.C.O., extension 481. I wasn't surprised when a secretary voice informed me that he wasn't in for the day. I wasn't surprised when his Solvay telephone rang for three minutes before I hung up. Then I cursed St. Johns, spent an hour hunting around auto supply shops for '65 Mercury parts, fixed the right tail light and headed north up Route 81 toward Davis Malloy's property in Belle Fredonia, seventy-five miles out of Syracuse.

It was mid-day, traffic lull time. I made it to Belle Fredonia in little more than an hour, despite the 55-mile speed limit newly tagged on by the fed government.

I had never been to Belle Fredonia, no tragedy in itself, but the fact left me unprepared for what greeted me. Instead of what I expected from a ville with such a grand name - upper-middle class semi-estates connected by private roads and well serviced by all the finer comforts of life that its pseudo-French name implied - I found instead an intersection-inspired farm town surrounded by land. Lots of land. Farm land and hunting land. Belle Fredonia, I discovered months later, had been founded by an English-hating French-Canadian who also hated nearby Fredonia. In an extended fit of pique he decided to use his many relations to set up a rival shop. Luciens and Clermonts seemed to abound in Belle Fredonia and, although

M'sieur Le Mayor died almost forty-five years ago, the accent was still French and the English belabored. I won the heart of Belle Fredonia's lone gas station attendant with a *"S'il vous plait, plein."*

As I waited for my *plein* tank of gas (BP, British Petroleum, ironically), the town's immediate economic situation opened before me: although no great shakes as a farming center, Belle Fredonia was a hunter's campground. Apparently autumn is the time for the *ville's* populace to shore up their collective financial foundation by catering to the primal needs and (not-so-primal) fantasies of the hunting season. In a town of only fifty buildings, you tend to notice three motels and five sport shops. I wondered how the Belle Fredonians felt about their two-months-a-year visitors.

The argument in front of the grocery store - Albany accent versus French - answered my speculation: typically Gallic.

Which didn't address my immediate problem: how to find Davis Malloy? I was at an unexpected dead end.

I had expected a local telephone book to be of assistance - there was none. Tracking down the Belle Fredonia edition of the Onondaga County phone directory only listed Malloy, Davis as being in Solvay; it did not even contain the alternate E.S.C.O office listing found in the Syracuse book.

Asking around proved false the traditional urban-rural dispute, i.e., that city people don't care about their neighbors while country folks are just one big happy family. No one I talked to in Belle Fredonia (and it wasn't very hard to hit about a quarter of the adult population within a five-minute walking radius) - nobody - had the slightest idea who Davis Malloy was. There was apparently no Sip 'n Sit within city limits.

Still, Lieutenant Anderson had found the elusive Davis Malloy here in Belle Fredonia just three days earlier. I could do the same. I headed for Town Hall.

The Town Hall of Belle Fredonia was small and simple, with all offices on the ground floor and all files in the basement. Following a serviceably helpful high school student, I descended into a grey concrete hole lit by unshaded light bulbs and lined on three of the four walls with brown metal file cabinets; the fourth wall oozed moisture from its porous, dank-smelling surface.

Feigning less helplessness than I felt, I induced the student to find me the files listing all property owners in Belle Fredonia. Paying him two dollars for the 'Use of Municipal Records' fee sent the student happily back to his Information Desk greeting post, where he could continue to point out to the ever-more-arriving guntoters that Belle Fredonia required

(*"C'est necessaire, m'sieur, necessaire"*) an additional 'Municipal Hunting' fee on top of the charge for the state hunting license. But I had my property files and that was all that was *necessaire* for me.

I didn't understand a thing I was reading.

Within minutes I was back upstairs at the Information Desk, juggling the three file folders I 'thought' might contain the information I sought and pestering the high school fountain of knowledge for help in deciphering the files.

"Eh bien," he muttered, and surrendered himself to the task.

"Eh bien," he re-muttered a moment later, then explained: "The property you're interested in, the... property of Davis Malloy...?"

"Davis Malloy," I echoed. "Yes, Davis Malloy."

"... is cross-filed at present, under his name and the name of the previous owner."

"Previous owner?"

"Yes, *alors,* you won't have to look for it, it's listed right... here," he pointed to a small asterisk, *"mais - s'il vous plait -* if you want, I can find you the file for the property year before it was sold to Monsieur..."

He talked on about old files, future files and cross-referenced cross-files. I didn't hear a word. I only stared at the asterisk indicating the previous owner of Davis Malloy's property. Behind that asterisk were the words: Eastern States Title Operators.

E.S.T.O.

chapter

twenty-two

The file with Davis Malloy's Belle Fredonia property information indicated no street address, only a map coordinate number.

Turning for assistance once again to the pride of the Belle Fredonia younger generation, I found the appropriate map and then, with less effort, the small square corresponding to Davis Malloy's property. According to the tax assessor's topographic map, it was an easily accessible plot of land, but only when guided by a knowledge of the local farm roads that my TEXACO COUNTRY special had failed to take into account.

By a fortunate coincidence, my Belle Fredonian town hall scholar informed me how, for only a small "Municipal Service" fee, I could have a photocopy made of the topographic map I was so admiring. I paid the kid a dollar for his literary abilities in title-reading, offered to be his silent partner if he ever went into business, and left the Town Hall carrying a greasy, blurred, photocopy of the map.

The farm roads, defying my expectations, were gravel-laid and well marked. Malloy's property was easily found fifteen minutes from town. Ten minutes from the nearest neighbor.

It was a wooded area - hunting land, not farm fields or orchards - which conveyed the impression of having once been a No Man's Land between the Hatfields and the McCoys. From the tax assessor's map description, I knew that the borders roughly transcribed a narrow rectangle on the area: deep, parallel streams cutting north to south delineated the property boundaries on those sides that did not abut a mountain or dirt road.

A barbed-wire fence ran along the inside banks of both those streams, apparently to keep the hunters out - not a bad idea if one wished to walk one's property without fear of gunshot wound during the autumn months. The arrangement was a not-uncommon one for upstate New York farm areas. Still, it didn't looked like Malloy's neighbors were encouraged to pay courtesy calls, either.

It was a small-sized piece of land. If you liked walking a quarter of a mile from where the road ended, along a wooded path to the cabin, it was almost minuscule. And the next half-mile past the cabin and into deeper woods was also easy to sneeze at. I hoped Malloy would be in his cabin so that I wouldn't have to court a cold finding out how easy.

In the distance, the faint sound of a tractor buzzed like a baritone hornet, probably laying under the fields before winter frost hardened the earth to concrete.

Halfway to Malloy's cabin I realized that I hadn't seen any other vehicles parked where I'd left mine at the end of the road. I doubled back to my car and surveyed the ground: it was the regular parking place, all right - oil spots, tire tracks and no other automobiles. Cursing myself on my deficient powers of observation that had me walking back and forth an extra quarter mile, I stomped up the path toward the cabin again, determined to press on with the hopeless sightseeing venture.

A bronze Maverick was parked next to the cabin. It was Anne Malloy's car.

I ran to the cabin. "Malloy!" I shouted, pounding on the door, "Davis Malloy!"

The cabin was locked and silent.

I ran to the car and checked the license plates - the same ones reported to me as Anne Malloy's when Bill Baeren had told me to watch her that night. The Maverick was scratched from coming up a path not meant for cars, its veneer spotted from the effects of sitting out in the open air for several days. No tire tracks, of course - grass will spring back after a few hours, let alone a few days. But why hadn't the police...?

... Who... didn't... know... about... the... car.

Anderson, when he visited Davis Malloy, could have been sitting on the hood of Anne Malloy's car eating his lunch and not known a thing about the Maverick's significance: I hadn't told him. Smart, smart me.

The car doors were locked. I was in no mood to let that stand in my way, but I still felt some reservations about breaking things. I held no reservations about "helping" things, though. I took my belt buckle, forced it between a window and the top rubber molding, and started jimmying the buckle up and down. Within a minute, the window had slid down a fraction and the rubber molding was torn away enough to allow me to put a finger through. Another minute later, I'd removed one of my shoelaces, tied it into a mini-lasso, and slipped it into the hole I'd made. Ten minutes later - not a good technique for car thieves, apropos, but effective in a clutch - I snagged the lock button. It lifted with a satisfying click, and I shot inside the car to rifle through the contents of its glove compartment.

The car registration was there. Made out to Davis Malloy.

chapter

twenty-three

Davis Malloy's cabin was next. This time I had no patience for the finer points of my sense of responsibility: I threw a rock through a window. Not a big rock. And a small window. A weekend in Purgatory. The combination got me inside.

The cold dampness of the unused cabin swept through me like fear. I stamped my feet in futile effort to dispel the chill running between my shoulder blades and pushed my thoughts into analytical mode. I've never been much of an observant scientist, so the thoughts devolved into sociological observation.

I have never figured out what distinguishes a 'cabin' from a 'shack'. If Malloy's full-time neighbors had lived in a one-room, fiberboard-walled construction with no electricity, running water or furniture they would have been eligible for federal aid for the underprivileged. Malloy's 'cabin' was no different than other weekend retreats I had been in: several cots, a card table and folding chairs, kerosene lamp and kerosene stove, empty bottles of alcohol stacked in one corner, full ones in another. When I was still a student who cared about those things, back in '69-'70 especially, it would have been the perfect place to go get high for the weekend. Now, I guessed (still not having made the transition to full-time grown-up), it was the rustic life that people retreated to after a hard week. I prefer the city. I have my own sunset to drink in front of.

The floor was concrete, a refinement I had not expected. I employed the floor as a striking surface for the match I used to light the kerosene lamp. I didn't know which was better to see by: the pale daylight with its shades-of-grey illumination filtering-in through the broken window, or the shadowy dullness of the lamp. I blew out the lamp. At least the daylight was unflickering.

Malloy had been here, I knew that from Anderson. Tuesday. And he'd been in Solvay on Thursday, I knew that from my phone call to him. But not "officially" - my guess was that Davis Malloy had picked up the phone from habit before remembering that he wasn't supposed to be "in".

The set-up of the cabin told me one other thing, something that I hadn't known beforehand - and I don't think Malloy had revealed to Anderson or the detective would have mentioned it: when Davis Malloy had been here last, he was not alone. There were two cots opened, each piled with sleep-disheveled blankets. That was the only thing the cabin told me.

It was enough to send me back to Solvay.

I rigged up a covering for the window I'd broken by hanging a blanket over a couple of nails pried from the wall. Then I crawled under the blanket and out the window, leaving the cabin locked and the impression of an unmolested property. At least from a distance. The wind blew gently and the blanket fell down. The broken window gaped open.

I let it stay.

I had other business.

Malloy or no Malloy, I was going to be a visitor in his home.

chapter

twenty-four

I telephoned Davis Malloy's home from the Sip 'n Sit. No answer. I went over to his house and received the same response. Then I drove back to my home, ate a large supper, slept for three hours, and returned to Solvay at 11:30 at night. I didn't expect Malloy to be in, but I drove by his house, just to check, on the off-chance that he was. No lights were on. No car was in the driveway. I knew from before that the garage was too crammed with household debris to hold a car.

No Davis Malloy.

I drove around the neighborhood till I found a house with three cars parked in front of it, then made mine the fourth. Without skipping a beat, I walked along the sidewalk to Malloy's house, up the driveway and around the side to the back door. A dog barked from the yard next door. I didn't try to quiet it. Instead, I leaned back into a corner and waited. A minute later, the dog's owner did what I couldn't have done.

Getting into the Malloy house was not difficult, although I was not prepared if it had been. I don't know a thing about picking locks or jimmying doors with crowbars quietly. I counted on the fact that most people, while locking and bolting their ground floor windows and doors, usually leave the second floor windows open a crack, especially in the bathroom. I didn't come by this insight through any "professional" experience: it's what my parents always did. When I was a teenager they'd sent me skittering up to the porch roof more than once to get us back into the house after we'd locked ourselves out.

Malloy's house was no exception. It even came equipped with a convenient patio roof and decorative wrought-iron trellis that allowed burglars and honest men alike to comfortably hoist themselves up to the second floor level. There were two windows open: the bathroom and the children's room. I opted for the bathroom.

I didn't know if it was a good idea or not, but I instinctually turned on the lights in every room I entered, leaving them on in the bedroom, kitchen and living room. I had a flashlight, but it struck me as rather obvious that a lone beam of light moving about inside a house would look more suspicious to burglar-conscious neighbors than an out-and-out attempt to make the place look lived-in. As long as no one remembered that Davis Malloy wasn't home.

I wanted photographs. Photographs of Anne Malloy. I wanted to see what her connection with Davis Malloy had been.

I found photographs - kid, Malloy and kid, Malloy, kid with clown, Malloy with kid and clown, many more, even photographs of the late Mrs. Malloy from four years before - the kid's name was Christy and the wife's name was Lorraine, I found that out, too - but I found nothing of Anne Malloy.

What I did find was confirmation of my first impressions: A family man. A man made alone by tragedy. A man justified in his actions. The house was not unusual. The photographs were. They were the illustrations of a sensitivity to the lives surrounding Davis Malloy. Almost a woman's sensitivity, despite the Irish maleness of his drinking.

I have since discovered that searching a house is not my forte. I didn't know it at the time. An hour-and-a-half of discreet closet ruffling and drawer shuffling produced nothing of relevance. I did not enter the kid's room. There could have been an elephant in there, I knew it at the time, but I wasn't going in. I hadn't become a ghoul yet. Instead, I ended my search where it should have begun, in a book-lined corner of the living room where a small table was strewn with letters and cards. Condolence cards. Letters of sympathy. And one that read from "Mother and Dad". An invitation to share his grief with his family. "Come home where you belong for now."

I turned to the book-lined wall that constituted Malloy's 'library' and searched out anything with maps. I found a road atlas, which I kept. Later, after sitting awhile and leafing through the atlas, I found the town of Chattleton, Alabama, twenty miles outside of Mobile. I was going there.

* * * * * * * *

I didn't have enough money to leave for Alabama the following morning, only two hundred and forty-eight dollars in my bank account. Not bad, but not enough for a four thousand mile car trip to Alabama and back.

My bank wouldn't give me a loan. So I withdrew what money I had, went to a savings bank, and deposited the money in a time account. Three days later, I borrowed two hundred dollars "on account." Five minutes after receiving the money, I walked up to a different cashier and withdrew my two-forty-eight time deposit, sacrificing the seven cents interest it had already accrued as a penalty for not maintaining my account for the minimum time required. Another two weeks in Purgatory; I was racking up the venial sins. I told the cashier I was proud to do business with such a large enterprise as theirs, then went home to pack, grateful for places where the wheels of bureaucracy and bookkeeping move exceedingly slow. I forgot to wonder if I had just committed bank fraud.

While I was waiting out the three days for the savings bank to process my account into their records, two things happened.

First, I paid an afternoon's visit to the Syracuse airport. An hour's walking the parking lot revealed Davis Malloy's Pontiac parked in the long-term, low-fee area. The ticket in the window dated it as the same afternoon I'd talked to him on the telephone. A quick check of the flight schedules and a longer chat with a cute-nosed, blue-eyed reservations clerk whose name badge said "Tina" indicated a daily flight to Washington, with connecting flights to Atlanta, Georgia and Birmingham, Alabama.

The second incident was a telephone call from Bill Baeren.

"Hello, Mark?"

There was the familiar accompaniment of chewed cheek muscles and flesh.

"I've been-" he started to whine.

I hung up on him.

"Bastard," I said.

I wished I had said it before hanging up.

I thought of these things while driving south.

chapter

twenty-five

It could have been a boring trip to Alabama, but I didn't let it. On the way I picked up five hitchhikers at various points - two were interesting, one talked my ear off, one slept, and one scared the hell out of me. The one that scared me, picked up somewhere in Pennsylvania and deposited (merciful Saint Christopher) in Baltimore, revealed casually that he was carrying a valise full of drugs. I declined to sample his wares, although he showed me his wealth to prove that he didn't need my "charity" and could pay his way if only I'd accept his currency. When I left him in Baltimore, he said he planned to get in touch with "the people."

One of the interesting hitchers was a girl heading for home and Kentucky. In exchange for pretending to be an English Lit. professor on my way to Florida, and an old friend of her boss, I was invited to spend the night with her family. The family turned out to be making its own trip at the time, visiting other relatives, so the alias was unnecessary. It was a good night. We sang songs together and danced.

I made the trip in five days. Although a born Yankee, I felt my tongue softening as I went further south. People would turn off when they saw the New York license plate - but they turned on again when I opened my mouth. By the time I hit Mobile, the accent was practically hometown, y'all know what ah mean.

* * * * * * * * *

Mobile, Alabama is a port city, with a sheltered access to the Gulf of Mexico growing more important monthly as dredges widen and deepen the channel to Mobile Bay. Early November now, it was a warm and radiant locale to a cold weather-tuned Northerner like myself. I packed away my sweaters on the first night.

I found Chattleton on the second night.

chapter

twenty-six

My first pass down Highway 75 missed Chattleton entirely. I didn't even know I'd missed it till I picked up a hitchhiker and told him I could only take him as far as Chattleton.

"Then y'all got to backtrack about two miles, mister."

I dropped him off at the Piggly Wiggly store he'd wanted to go to, headed back up the road towards Mobile and missed Chattleton again.

I found it on the third try.

There wasn't much to miss in Chattleton, Alabama, at least not from what was visible from the highway: two stores and a gas station. No signs saying 'Welcome to Chattleton' or 'You are now leaving Chattleton.' My cue that I was there came only from the gold letters on the back of a jacketed teenager, letters proclaiming Chattleton Drum and Bugle Corps. Five minutes and a bottle of Orange Crush later, I was driving the owner of that jacket down an offshoot of the highway that led to the Chattleton post office. Mrs. Lawrence (Elaine) Malloy, postmistress, would be closing up shop there at about 7 p.m.

"Well, y'all never cain tell if he wants his mail er not. G'wan down ta his house tomorra mornin' before comin' here 'n tell him his letter box hasn't been emptied out 'n three weeks. Tell'm if he wants me ta throw t'all out, all he's gotta do is leave it here one more day."

The voice that greeted me as I entered the post office was high and cliché. It came from behind the wall of post boxes that greeted visitors just inside the door, and when it stopped droning I expected to see a faithful minion of the postal service scuttle out to follow his postmistress's orders. Instead, I heard a telephone receiver click down with a heavy hand and a string-beaned cartoon woman come scuttling out instead.

Mrs. Lawrence (Elaine) Malloy had probably been prettier in her youth, but I doubted it was to any degree. Time, meanwhile, had taken what must have been plain features and sharpened them into a caricature of a face, her nose literally ski-sloping over a mouth permanently sour-pussed. A smile indicating her recognition of my presence merely increased her likeness to Stan Laurel.

"Excuse me, ma'am. Are you Mrs. Malloy?"

"What can I do for you?" she said professionally, modulating her accent to reflect my own. In other words, she apparently talked rube to the yokels and English to the rest of us. "May I help you?" she asked again helpfully.

The teenager shouted through the screen door,

"He's from New York, Aunt Elaine. I helped him find y'all."

"All right, Glenn Ray. I'll take care of him. Thank you." The high voice took on a certain particular motherly quality, the one I'd always been happy not to be subjected to.

She turned another cartoon smile to me. "Where y'all from Mister... ?"

"Cornell. Mark Cornell."

"Jewish?" She stared at my nose which, having been broken three times, probably fulfilled her expectations.

"Catholic mutt," I answered.

A slight frown of disillusion made a quick appearance, then was erased by a flash of inspiration: "Just about the same thing, not quite Christian." That resolved, she smiled. "Mr. Cornell. I have a boy from up in Syracuse, New York."

"I know. I came to see him."

There was a plaque on the far wall under a poster of the newest commemorative stamp. The plaque proclaimed that Elaine Malloy had scored 98 out of a possible 100 on her examination for postmistress. I had taken the postal examination once, a few years before. The entrance-level exam. I scored 85.

Mrs. Malloy had been talking while I read the plaque. She had been lying, so I ignored her. When she stopped talking, I read the poster above the plaque. When I finished reading the poster, I read the plaque again. The high score made me jealous. Mrs. Malloy didn't like my reading habits. She told me so.

"Mr. Cornell, I'm not accustomed to being ignored when I'm talking to a person!"

I looked at her with as much innocence as I could muster.

"I'm sorry," I said, "but I believe your son bought airplane tickets to Washington and Birmingham."

"You know my son?"

"I assumed he came here." I didn't like the taste in my mouth. The Orange Crush had been warm.

I added, "Especially after the murder of his wife."

She looked at me as if all the grief in the world had suddenly been laid on her shoulders. Of course, I was the one laying it on - she couldn't refrain from telling me that.

"Why are you being so cruel, Mr. Cornell?"

"I'm not. I was truly concerned about his wife's death."

"My son's wife died four years ago." She tried to look serious and tragic. It only annoyed me.

"And I know his son's dead, Mrs. Malloy." I didn't want to see her much longer. "I need to talk with your son. Maybe I can help."

"Cousin Dave was down by the gas station just a half hour ago," the teenager's voice piped-in through the screen door, letting curiosity overcome fear of his aunt. "Y'all a detective, Mr. Cornell?"

"In everything but my dreams," I answered.

"I think I'd better take you to meet Davis' father," said a distrustful tart-faced cartoon, casting a dour eye upon her treacherous nephew. I expected he would receive little mail in the months to come.

Funny thing about my just-ended conversation with Elaine Malloy, though: for all her concern over "Davis's tragedies" and her "poor dead grandson," she never asked me what the hell did I mean when I said "the murder of his wife."

chapter

twenty-seven

It wasn't easy to follow Elaine Malloy down the night-graying back roads. Hard enough to follow her dark green car in the twilight, Mrs. Malloy seemed inclined to lose me in a swirl of dust if the opportunity could be arranged. If she'd known a quick turn-off she could have done it: the forest on either side of the roads was impenetrable beyond ten yards. Although the underbrush was the brown-yellow dead of autumn, the forest was dominated by fir trees. Blue. I followed her tail lights, their red dots the only contrast to the blurring forest, road and dusk.

Her house was a rambling one-story construction with a screen-enclosed patio porch half-again as big as the house. Only the kitchen light was on, giving the structure a deserted look, like when a family goes on vacation and leaves its porch light on to "make burglars think we're at home" - at three in the afternoon.

Mrs. Malloy was out of her car and slamming the kitchen door behind her before I'd brought my car to a complete stop. As she entered, the kitchen light was immediately obscured by the silhouette of a man, a man whose features were clearly outlined as he moved over to the refrigerator and behind the light. He opened the refrigerator and calmly poured something, listening in abstract silence, while the cliché voice rattled unintelligible phrases.

I waited in my car a moment, then walked over to the garage. It was a two-car garage, half-filled by a pick-up truck. But there had been no room inside for Mrs. Malloy's car because a rented sedan with Birmingham, Alabama license plates occupied the second half. I went to the kitchen door and knocked.

"Y'all wait there. I'll let y'all in. But you wait till I'm ready!" scrambled a cartoon character.

"Come on in," countermanded a low, steady voice. "You can open a door."

The voice was neither friendly nor unfriendly. It certainly wasn't inviting me in for a good time; but it took me off the defensive - too far off the defensive.

I entered the kitchen and walked over to the man sitting at the formica-topped kitchen table, secure behind a gallon-sized plastic milk bottle holding some volatile liquid. Lawrence Malloy. He rose and extended a hand. It wasn't until I'd grabbed it that

I realized his little finger was missing, cut off at the knuckle. I made to relax my grip, but he held firm.

"Hit doesn't hurt," he said. "'Lost hit last year, but hit doesn't hurt." Finally he loosened his grip and we let our hands fall. We remained standing.

"'Man wants a drink, Elaine," he said without looking back. "You bring me a glass for Mr. Cornell."

He unscrewed the top of the milk bottle and bestowed upon me a drink slightly smaller than the Gulf of Mexico. He poured himself a Caribbean Sea. It bothered me vaguely that the stuff in my glass smelled like a first cousin to gasoline; it also looked like piss. Lawrence Malloy noticed my discomfort and mentioned that the plastic bottle had a tendency to leech into the alcohol -

"Don't worry about it, though: nobody ever got cancer or anything - just don't let it set in your mouth too long."

I was not overly reassured.

"Sit down, Mr. Cornell. Elaine has to fix supper. She won't be needin' that chair."

Standing, he was a good six inches shorter than I. Six inches shorter and thirty years stronger. Sitting, Lawrence Malloy was my height. Behind a bottle he merely looked old. He had strong eyes, though, like his son's. We drank silently to start the conversation. I nearly died when it hit my throat.

Davis Malloy's father leaned to one side and tapped the plastic milk bottle, smiling at my discomfort.

"Y'all probably didn't notice the shitty lookin' trap of a house a half-mile or so back, but they're the producers of this brand of 'Walker Red. They're millionaires, y'all know that?" His voice hadn't missed a beat, and he had gulped down two healthy mouthfuls during the sentence. "Hit's true, Mr. Cornell." A good, solid voice. His smile started tightening. "They'd be even richer if they'd stay off of United Paper Company land." A voice that talked to itself a lot. "The bastards don't realize that if I'm mapping company land and find their equipment, I've got to do my job." A justified voice. "I gave hit back to 'em two times. Can't do it a third and a fourth." A voice belonging to a man who preferred to be alone days.

He tapped the plastic milk bottle again, setting the yellow liquid inside to jiggling the light beams running through it. "They make a good product, though."

Elaine Malloy's cartoon voice popped in: "Lawrence, why don't y'all talk about Davis? This man's come to torment Davis. Davis is too fine to-"

"Because I talk to a man the way a man talks, dammit!"

She walked out of the kitchen and I was glad.

Malloy's father turned to me: "I shouldn't have talked to her like that and she was right. What do y'all want to see Davis for?"

He didn't seem like a guy to lie to. So I didn't exactly lie: I told him what Ray St. Johns firmly believed:

"Because I think he's trying to kill the wrong man."

Unpleasant surprise registered in the old man's face, then an almost-pride.

Coupled with suspicion.

"You told Elaine a different story an hour ago."

"It's the same story, only different parts."

"Tell me all the parts, then."

"All right."

I gave him a theory, an attractive one.

"A couple of weeks ago your son's wife, Anne, was thrown out of an apartment window and killed, the day after your grandson died. Davis," I tried to sound familiar, "found out that a black man was in the same apartment. My guess is that your son figured this black man killed her. So Davis tried to kill the black guy. In a bar. Only he missed and killed someone else. He tried again, only the black guy was lucky again. It was only luck. Your son planned his revenge well enough, though: nobody even knows it was him shooting up the bar. Except for me and a guy sitting in jail in Syracuse."

Malloy's father practiced his abstract silence on me for a while instead of his wife, finally asking absently, "Why are you here?"

"I just want to talk to your son. I understand why he tried to kill the guy. I understand why he ran away from Syracuse."

The old man motioned to the stove: "Turn off the gas, will you?" As I walked over to turn off the fire under a pan of burning french fries, he added, "Only one thing wrong with your story, Mr. Cornell: my son's wife died four years ago; her name wasn't 'Anne'."

"I know."

He looked at me awkwardly. The whole kitchen grew awkwardly silent. I heard a quick-rhythmed breathing coming from the living room. After a moment, so did Malloy's father. It annoyed him into words, loud enough for his wife to hear without straining.

"And Davis wouldn't kill nobody, either. He's strong enough not to kill."

"I wouldn't know." I said, telling the full truth now: "I've never really met your son. Seen him once. Talked to him. He never talked back. Don't know him at all. 'Just saw the woman called 'Anne Malloy' get shoved out a window and die. And your son Davis hired the guy who hired me to watch her: 'said she was his wife and she was committing adultery and I was supposed to watch who she was sleeping with. That's all I know. I don't know Davis."

Lawrence Malloy stared at me. I couldn't tell if he thought I was lying, was a crazy man, the devil - or telling him something he already knew about. His face was impassive and he shifted his eyes down to look at where his missing finger had been. I knew this: he could out-silence me any time. He'd been practicing all his life. I even felt a little sorry for his wife: whatever else, it had to be a lonely marriage.

I was also starting to feel sleepy from the alcohol. I knew that I'd surpassed my hard stuff limit by half a glass. What the hell, I figured, it'll do me no good to talk to Davis Malloy right now, I'll fall asleep in his face. I'll be lucky if I don't run off the road on the way back to Mobile. I decided to leave.

"Excuse me," I said, crossing the kitchen, "I'll be back tomorrow."

Lawrence Malloy made no attempt to stop me.

But I didn't leave - at least not back to Mobile.

As I crossed the yard to my car, a red glow filled the night sky from some spot down the road about a mile away.

Malloy's father, watching me leave through the kitchen screen door, saw the red glow, too. As he ran toward his pick-up truck parked in the garage, we could hear the distant, country-clear echoes of a gunned motor.

Then a sound that reminded me of nightmares about Flora's bar and Ray St. Johns: the rapid fire of several shotgun blasts.

chapter

twenty-eight

I followed Lawrence Malloy's truck deeper into the backwoods as closely as I could, which wasn't too close considering the speeds the pick-up was hitting. I didn't know the road and had no intention of being a hero. But it was only a mile we traveled, and then, suddenly, I found my car breaking into a clearing. For at least a square mile the forest was cleared away: a gentle rolling pasture land took its place.

Pasture land littered with the shadows of dead cattle and lit by the bright sun of a burning barn.

The pick-up truck had stopped in mid-field next to a nervous girl astride an even more nervous horse. She was shouting something, but I only caught the final "... Davis is following to get the license number!"

Then the pick-up spit dirt from its rear wheels and arrowed towards the barn.

The girl slapped hard at her horse with the reins, urging him to follow. The stallion would not stop his nervous circling. Finally, she leapt to the ground and ran towards the barn.

I shifted into second gear and caught up with her halfway there. I didn't need to say anything: as soon as I pulled alongside her she opened the car door and jumped in. I don't think she even closed the door. A minute later, close to the barn, she popped out of the car before I was fully stopped.

Lawrence Malloy stood at the barn door, prying at a padlock with a tire iron. Inside, the cattle that had been locked-in cried out in terror and pain. It was like individual voices pleading for help. I could smell them burning.

I could also tell that on the inside of the barn the air was so hot that - if the door were opened - anyone standing there would be seared to the flesh. Malloy's father and the girl were attacking the lock together now. They would have it broken before I could run to them.

I watched them work on, pushing towards disaster, panic-stricken for the second time in my experience with Malloys. I thought of Anne Malloy. I thought of her face. I thought of burned faces. I pounded on the car horn in frustration.

They heard it and hesitated.

I pounded again. They went back to forcing the door open. Again. They ignored me.

I started the car in a grind of nervous gears and aimed at the two figures worrying the padlock preparatory to a final assault. They tried to ignore me, but did not succeed for long. I hit them, jamming on the brakes at the same time, knocking Lawrence Malloy and the girl against the hot barn door. It burned to the touch, but it was still a closed door. Angrily, pained by the blistering wall, they stumbled out of my way. I pushed the car bumper flat against the door.

"Get out of here! Out of here!" I yelled. I could feel the heat wrap around my windshield and pound in through the open side windows. "Get out!"

The pleas of the cattle were only a yard, two yards, away. On the other side of a closed door. But that door was all that kept the skin over my flesh. I could smell the cattle's burning hair and flesh, fire-bursting hay, boiling urine, fried shit. "Get away!" I began crying.

Malloy's father was the first to realize what I meant. He grabbed the girl by an elbow and pulled her back to the safety of his pick-up. He waited there a moment, then ran over to my car and opened the driver's-side door. The paint finish was beginning to bubble on the nose of the hood.

"Move over," the solid voice said, "You've got too much smoke in your eyes to drive."

* * * * * * * * *

We sat in the pick-up for half an hour, watching a beautiful fire with horrible sounds coming from it. I think we each took turns crying. From the smoke. There wasn't much to talk about. The girl's horse came over to the truck and paced around it a while, looking to us for protection, but scared of the death nearby. Finally, the horse cantered into the dark.

"He'll be back at the house when we get there," said Malloy's father, breaking the silence and whatever comfort it had wrought.

There were no sounds coming from the barn by then. There hadn't been for ten minutes. In their place, now, we could hear occasional moans of distress from the cattle in the fields: every one had been shotgun blasted, not all had been killed.

The old man reached across the girl's lap, fumbled about in the cluttered glove compartment, and took out a box of rifle shells. Then he turned in his seat, reached over my head, and unstrapped a rifle fixed onto the back of the cab. He left us sitting there.

Five minutes later came the sound of a rifle shot. A minute later, another. I found myself hugging a crying girl next to me. I wanted someone to hug me. There were eleven shots in all. Then the night was quiet. I couldn't see into the dark. The contrast with the bright light from the barn made it too difficult.

"Why don't you take Linda back to the house?"

The voice startled me. Lawrence Malloy was opening the door to the cab.

"I'll wait here for Davis," he added.

"I-"

"I'll wait here for Davis."

"Yessir."

I don't know why I said that. It seemed natural.

I walked with the no longer crying girl closer to the barn. The roof had collapsed, releasing the building's pent-up heat into the sky. A slight wind at our backs made it possible to stand relatively close to the blazing structure. It stank of ugly things, but we were used to the smell by then. We stared stupidly at the fire-twisted metal padlock a moment, then turned and headed for my car. As we got in, Malloy's father shouted from the pick-up, "Linda, tell your mother to bring my jacket!"

I looked to the girl: "I can get it and bring it back. Or he can have mine."

I reached over to the back seat for my windbreaker.

"He wants Momma," the girl said.

chapter

twenty-nine

Mrs. Malloy was on the telephone when we arrived; I could see her through the kitchen door. She hung up as we walked from the car to the house.

"Davis has got the fire department and the police coming," she said to her daughter, pointedly ignoring me. "They'll be here in five, ten minutes... He didn't get the license plate number."

Linda Malloy spat out the words, "No big question about that, is there?"

"No. I could go down the road a half mile and tell 'em what the license plate number is tomorrow."

"Daddy wants his jacket, Momma."

The cartoon woman pulled the waiting jacket off the back of a kitchen chair. She didn't skip a beat from her earlier statement. "But I can't say I saw it happen. I can't say I saw it." She looked at me as if she wanted to blame me, decided against it, and walked quickly out of the house. We could hear the steady sound of her car ignition, followed by a quick but unhurried growl of acceleration as she left the drive and disappeared down the road.

Linda Malloy turned to me. "Y'all want something to eat?"

"Not for a week."

"Yeah... Well, I'll make something to drink."

"No alcohol, please. And my name's Mark Cornell."

She looked a little disconcerted that we had been together for so long and she hadn't asked my name. She was even more ill-at-ease when I added, "Your father already told me yours."

A pair of pale brown eyes suddenly reminded me that I was talking with Davis Malloy's sister and that, after she talked with her parents, she was probably not going to like me very much. I took a close look at the sweat-stained woman making coffee and plunged in.

Not a deep plunge at first.

"You know who killed those cattle?"

"Our cattle, Mr. Cornell."

"Mark."

"Mark. Our cattle: Daddy had that land before he started working for the United Paper Company, back before World War Two. People know that. Just ask the last whiskey-makin' operation he busted up."

"You mean the people down the road? The millionaire moonshiners?"

A dirty blond head struggled through a polyester pullover windbreaker being taken off. Electricity made her hair crackle a little as she smoothed it back with a free hand. The other hand gave me a thumbs-up "You got it" sign.

"What happened with you and your brother? Why were you two there?"

"We were riding, that's all, and we-"

Suddenly she bolted out of the kitchen and into the dark, slamming the screen door in her wake.

I was halfway into the yard behind her when she stopped at the sound of a horse snorting, a sound coming from a building off to the side of the garage. Linda Malloy stood stock still for a moment - then started shaking with relief. I stepped up close to offer her the same shoulder to lean against she'd shared when we were in the pick-up together, but she held her arms up and warded me off, walking in tight circles around the yard and breathing deeply to slow down the shakes.

"I guess Momma took care of Johnny B.," she said after a while.

"Who?"

"Johnny B. Good, my-"

"-horse," I remembered.

"I was afraid he'd be..."

She didn't need to say more: "shot, too" were the words we both used in our imaginations to finish the sentence.

We walked back toward the house, some of the tension of the past hour broken at last.

"It's my horse," she opened the door and motioned me in, "my horse, my house, my land - it would have been my cattle, too, but..."

Water takes a long time to boil. We stood staring at the gas fire ring under the kettle. She continued:

"Davis left. Fifteen years ago. So it's all gonna be mine." I busied myself with finding coffee cups. "Of course, anything he wants is his, but he left it, he said."

She found two coffee cups sitting in the sink. "'Mind?" she asked, indicating them.

"Nope."

She rinsed them out a little less than I would have liked. Then we stood back and waited some more for the water to boil.

"Did you see it happen?"

She shook her head. "Only the end, 'coupla minutes before y'all got there."

I needed to bring the questions to topics that would get me kicked out of the house if her mother returned.

"'You ever visit your brother? Up north?" I tried to make it sound more casual than I felt.

She answered matter-of-factly: "I lived with him for three years. I took care of little Christy after his wife Lorraine died.

"I left too soon."

She was in a pleasant melancholy, a melancholy that made her face look fine-boned and thoughtful. Almost a stylized drawing of an intelligent woman. It seemed that all of the Malloys bore an aura of animation.

"I want to break things - fuck!" she said in a low, firm voice reminiscent of her father's, thus shattering the image I had been creating for her of a sad, soulful woman.

Her pleasant melancholy faded and she turned her attention to me.

"I know your accent," she said. "You're from Syracuse. I was there too long not to recognize it."

"Why did you leave?" I asked.

"Because my father had an accident. And because..."

She stopped talking before the water came to a boil, but the shrill whistle of the kettle was a convenient excuse for her not to continue. I didn't know how to ask the follow-up questions, and she didn't seem to want to talk about it, so I pulled back and hoped she start up on her own again.

I found the sugar while she filled our two cups with instant coffee, pouring the finally-boiling water over the 'freeze-dried' imitation of taste.

We didn't say much for a while. Linda looked at me, not wanting to give out her life story to a stranger, and I looked at the sugar in the bottom of my coffee cup, hoping she would not ask me why I was being so nosy.

It wasn't very uncomfortable, though. Not after the barn. Not after the cattle. Two people who've been scared and cried together either don't want to see the other ever again - or trust one another. Sometimes they trust strangers. Sometimes they trust the other too much. I pushed.

"Did you know Anne?"

Blank stare.

"Anne?"

Blank stare. Answer:

"I left because my brother wanted me to keep on playing housewife. He didn't need other women when I was around. I didn't know about Christy having cancer until a month ago or I would have gone back... But then, neither did Davis."

"He didn't know his son was dying of cancer?"

"Some kind of cancer where the symptoms don't show so much."

"Leukemia?"

She nodded.

"Why is he here now?"

"Why do you think?"

It was getting chilly. No one had closed the kitchen door to the outside, only the screen door. I went over and switched on a burner on the gas stove, warming my hands over the flame.

"Tired?" I asked.

"Not particularly."

"I can come back tomorrow and see your brother."

"I'm waiting up for him 'n Momma 'n Dad anyway. You can stay."

"I'll be back tomorrow."

She crossed over to the formica table and slumped in a chair as I turned and headed for the door.

"Are you a detective, Mark?"

I was supposed to be surprised by the question, but I was too tired. My answer even was basically the truth when she said, "I'm gonna repeat the question 'Are you a detective, Mark?'"

"For myself. What are you?"

She must have been too tired to lie, too - she didn't skip a beat before saying dully:

"I'm nothing now. I used to be a college student when I lived in Solvay. Photography at S.U."

"I'll see you tomorrow," I said and walked out the door. Then I tried to drive the 20 miles to my motel in Mobile and ended up sleeping in a truck stop pullover as the next best thing to falling asleep and ramming into a tree. Before I slept troubled dreams, though, I made an important stop.

* * * * * * * * *

My eyes were stinging from the smoke and my mouth was bitterly dry. Pulling out of the Malloys' drive, I remembered that I had a cup of untasted coffee sitting on a kitchen table not fifty yards away. Let it stay, I thought, I've made my exit. I even made it gracefully. It was an accomplishment which, considering the situation, was a stroke of luck probably not to be repeated. But I was in no condition to go speeding back to Mobile, fancy exit or no. Especially over a dirt road that I'd only gone over once. Hunched behind the steering wheel, windows open in a vain attempt to chill myself awake, I drove slowly toward the highway leading back to the city.

About a half mile down the road I passed a flatboard house. I noticed it only because the lights were on and a television was broadcasting loud enough for world reception. A dog made a half-hearted attempt to chase my car, more as a matter of form than from interest, then galloped off into the forest undergrowth after smaller and faster prey. A hundred yards past the house, I pulled over to the side of the road and stopped my car. I could hear the dog barking somewhere in the forest at right angles to the road. When he sounded far enough away for my peace of mind, I got out of the car and backtracked to the flatboard house.

Lawrence Malloy had understated his case: the "shitty lookin' trap of a house" the moonshiners inhabited didn't even rate the title of "house" to my mind - "shack" would have been my kindest nominative, though any building with as much green fungus crudding up its walls as this one had would be best described as a "hole". From the exterior. Despite emissions of a strong odor reminiscent of ripe compost heaps, what I could see through the open window indicated a considerably more lavish interior decor. Apparently the local whiskey kings did not believe in lording it over their neighbors in too-apparent fashion. Still, the creature comforts of a twenty-five inch color television console and a wall-filling stereo ensemble tended to set off the wall-to-wall carpeting on which the occupants were lounging rather comfortably. I didn't feel like going closer to discover what other luxuries they employed, I was jealous enough as it was.

There were three cars parked behind the house: two representing a male and female sex fantasy apiece, plus a third representing my reason for being there - a van. The kind of van that one delivers multi-gallon orders of bootleg in, or drives over rough terrain. The vehicle they would have used when butchering Lawrence Malloy's cattle. And the piece of evidence I needed to examine in order to check out a developing theory of mine. Not evidence for the police, just confirmation of a theory.

The first point of my examination aimed directly at the inhabitants of the house I was prowling around - and put my theory on shaky ground: the engine of the van was warm. Not hot to the touch, no, but it had been driven about an hour before.

The second point of my examination confirmed my theory, though. I checked the tires of the van. The treads were clogged with dirt, gravel and asphalt, but all was old, dry. I have yet to see a car that can drive over the wet grass of pasture land, land frequently ankle-deep in cow feces, and retain no traces of the journey.

This van had not been off the normal roads that night.

I walked quickly around the flatboard house and back onto the road, heading toward my car with an exaggerated quick-walk that kept breaking into a skip. Almost there, a dog burst out of the forest and took a snap at my leg, quietly, not barking like before. He liked slower game now, I supposed. He caught me before I had a chance to be surprised, biting the side of my knee to the bone. I really didn't feel much. The dog bit, let go as quickly as he came, then trotted off down the road toward his home. When he got to the yard, he turned and started barking at me.

By that time I was in my car and didn't care - my knee was starting to throb and my hands were less than firm on the steering wheel. I pulled out too quickly, skidded a bit on the gravel, and squinted my way down the black night dirt road until I hit the highway.

chapter

thirty

Waking up at seven the next morning was not an easily accomplished task. The will was there, but the power was not. When my travel clock brayed its announcement of appointed time, I waited out the twenty-five seconds it took for the alarm's spring to run down, then went back to sleep.

Unfortunately, I had been too good a judge of my own character the night before and had requested at the motel desk to be awakened at seven-thirty. The rotten efficiency experts employed there did it, too, not even allowing a decent thirty-second fudge interval, but telephoning my room at precisely the half-hour. Then they phoned again five minutes later to inquire whether or not I desired room service to bring me breakfast. Having neither the money nor the strength to pursue such a desire, I resisted the impulse to request a public hanging of all desk personnel as a side order to bacon and eggs and simply declined breakfast altogether.

Not that I didn't eat breakfast. Within ten minutes an electric pot was boiling water while a hungry New York visitor to Mobile was consuming butter-fried eggs with toast - the wonders of a portable camp stove bought long ago to overcome the indigestion of on-the-road dining. A decision of Palate and Budget. At any rate, the process woke me up and kept my mind occupied enough not to be made sick again by memories of the night before.

* * * * * * * * *

The memories were given a new freshness when I returned to the Malloys' place later that morning.

Following the dusty wake of a trailer-van down the back road of Chattleton that led to their house, I turned off at the Malloys' drive expecting to find someone at home. I didn't have time to turn off the car engine before a quick glance revealed a deserted garage and empty stables. Perhaps someone was in the house, but it had that cold look of a building that has no occupants while being open all the night. I backed out of the drive and followed in the direction of the trailer-van.

A dead autumn sun illuminated the pasture land and added a photographic quality of false light to the scene of business. Four trailer-vans were driving around the field, stopping wherever a man in blood-stained coveralls would direct them. Once stopped, two men in equally blood-stained clothing would jump out of the cab, run over to one of the dead cattle and tug the corpse onto the automatic lift of the trailer. They were only picking up the animals that had been shot. Apparently, the coveralled director of the trailer-vans was grading the cattle according to quality, for hides or meat I couldn't tell.

Lawrence Malloy walked alongside the man, arguing quietly on occasion, downgrading even the assessor's valuation more than once. His wife walked behind them both, calculating the assessor's estimations on a pocket computer. I couldn't make out a word any of them said, only the gestures, but her high voice carried across the field, adding an annoying keen that worked as an antidote to any feelings of horror the scene may have evoked. It became instead a stench-filled business activity that left one unaffected by the mutilation it revolved about. Maybe that was the idea. The Banality of Commerce in triumph over Evil and that kind of philosophical crap. (Not a big surprise that I was not a very successful Philosophy major for that one, brief flameout of a semester.)

The barn was a part of the activity, too, but separate in that it apparently had already been picked clean of commercial value. A pile of blackened metal objects - tools, troughs, tractor hook-ups - had been salvaged from the structure, heaped to the side and tagged with a cardboard sign marked "Scrap Pik UP". The barn was still standing, at least in outline. It was a shaky outline, though, one that crumbled like a chalkboard drawing when a bulldozer warily edged into a corner of it. The rafter toppled inward, and after a few jolts on each corner there was nothing left standing higher than a man's height. The bulldozer began to push the wreckage into a deep trench dug along the length side of the barn, a trench that had not been there the night before. The operator of the machine worked slowly but steadily, and within minutes the larger portion of what had been a barn and cattle was out of sight. Linda Malloy rode her horse Johnny B. Goode around the whole lot, watching with eyes deader than the ashes.

Occasionally, as the bulldozer pushed into a pile of blackened debris, a bright red patch would appear, the cracked, burnt hide of one of the dead cattle breaking open and revealing the uncooked flesh beneath. Linda's horse would shy away at the smell that accompanied the bursting color. After a few such jumpbacks, one nearly tumbling them both over, she dismounted Johnny B. and stood near the barn holding the horse by his reins. He was still nervous, she nearly motionless.

Davis Malloy was not in sight.

I stayed in my car at the edge of the pasture for twenty minutes, maybe thirty. Lawrence Malloy acknowledged my presence with a look, his wife with a non-seeing look, and Linda Malloy with a raised middle finger. She ignored me for the remainder of my vigil until, as I revived the engine and started turning to go back to their house, I saw her reflection in my rear view mirror, mounting the horse and cantering down the hill in my direction. I turned off the engine and waited.

"Talked to your folks, didn't you?" I said as she drew alongside.

"Um-hmmm," she hummed musically.

"Talk to your brother?"

"Not about you. He was too busy helping Daddy and Momma get through this."

"They don't look too broken up about it," I said, not believing it as I said it. The high-pitched voice of Mrs. Malloy wasn't counting any numbers, it was crying in the only way she knew how. But it was still annoying. I pushed on.

"Where's your brother?"

Linda Malloy cantered past me down the road.

Obviously, diplomacy would have been a better policy than smart-assed cracks. I let her have a five minute start, then drove down the road after her. She got to the house before I did. She was standing in her front lawn, holding her horse by the reins.

She was also talking with her brother.

chapter

thirty-one

Linda Malloy gave a start of surprise when I pulled into the driveway. "Surprise"? - yeah, I guess that's what you have to call it, although it was more like the look given a dentist entering his own office to fill your tooth, an expression of inevitable unpleasantness, than a reaction to the unexpected. She knew I would be coming, just didn't expect it so soon.

Linda stayed long enough to introduce me to her brother, then led her horse over to the stable. Another horse was quartered inside already, one that hadn't been there when I'd first come by. Davis Malloy's horse I suppose. I've never cared to ask him.

The strong features of Davis Malloy's face seemed unchanging as he stated, "My sister tells me you're from Syracuse, Mr. Cornell."

"Born there."

A slight smile caught at the corners of his mouth.

"What do you do there, Mr. Cornell?"

"Real estate appraiser. You ever hear of E.S.T.O.?"

The smile stayed caught where it was.

"I'd have to be blind not to," he said, a second too late. "Half the housing developments around Syracuse are stamped from the E.S.T.O. cookie cutter." The smile was still in place, friendly, but tentative. "Mine was too."

"Mine, too," I laughed. I saw Linda Malloy walking toward us. "Of course, I'm an apartment dweller myself - and an apartment appraiser, too."

Her dark blond hair was caught back by a flat barrette into a duck's tail. Linda Malloy looked at her brother, then stood nearer to him as she turned her look toward me. "You told me you were a detective, Mr. Cornell," she accused.

"Mark," I corrected, catching her off-guard and making Linda turn sheepishly to her brother like an apologetic puppy returning to its master after accepting food from a stranger.

"But it's the same," I continued, turning my attention back to her brother. "I was appraising a certain apartment on Salina Street a few weeks ago when Anne was killed."

Davis Malloy took his sister's hand. One of them was comforting the other, but I couldn't tell who.

"What were you appraising in the apartment, Mr. Cornell?" he asked. His voice carried an undertone of strong emotion.

I lied then. I lied because I wanted to ask flat out what was going on and I knew I couldn't. I lied in the plausible direction left to me.

"I was appraising the electrical system, Mr. Malloy."

Pause: one, two, three, four, five.

"Do you know everything about it?" Malloy asked vaguely.

"It's on record with my business associates."

Linda Malloy cut in. "He said you tried to kill a man, Davis. That's what he told Daddy. He said it was about some woman named Anne who was your wife." She was confused. So was I. I waited for her brother's reaction.

When the reaction finally came, it was cryptic, confusing and embarrassingly emotional at once.

"...The business associates," he said to an invisible mirror image of himself, repeating my earlier words, but not quite. There was another slight difference between what the two of us said: I had been walking around a lie - I knew Bill Baeren had destroyed every record of Davis Malloy's visit to his office - but Davis was stepping closer to the truth. "… business … associates," he repeated with a mumble. His face, still dignified, seemed to mask a crumbling inside.

Then a shudder passed through his body. Forcibly, Davis Malloy made an effort not to weep, but his eyes gazed at me through a film of water he could not control. His words were still steady, but there was a slight gurgling catch to his speech.

"My wife died four years ago," he explained tersely. He wanted to move, I wanted to move, but we didn't. "And my son died two weeks ago. Your business associates… know that," he said. "They know that."

I may have said something next, I planned to push the grieving husband-and-father, because his emotions seemed, somehow, "inappropriate." But I needed a moment to get over my growing dislike of Davis Malloy and phrase the next questions without emotion. Before I could do that, the opportunity was taken away.

A dark green car pulled into the drive, his mother's car with his father behind the wheel and his mother, calculator in hand, seated cartoon-faced beside him.

The small triangle of Linda, Davis and myself remained intact as the car pulled up across the yard, but the spell of intimate secrets and threats was broken. Davis Malloy uncrumbled his inner self, stepped out of our triangle and walked over to his mother's door, opening it before she could.

"Let's fix somethin' to eat," he said, putting an arm around her shoulder. He was a perfect son, a damn well respectable man. "Dad, why don't you get some rest?"

"No," said the old man, rubbing the hand with the little finger missing. "I'll take a shit, then hike on down the road and get my truck." Lawrence Malloy let his son lead the family matriarch into the house - a fine performance of filial piety - then headed in himself. He stopped at the door and looked over at me: "Y'all can wait around a minute an' give me a ride, right?"

Davis Malloy and his mother were already in the house. Linda tried to discourage the suggestion.

"I could-" she began.

"I don't mind," I said quickly. "I'll wait out here."

"OK," nodded Lawrence Malloy. "And since I'll have a bit a time, then, I'll eat a little something first. Y'all don't mind waiting?"

"No."

"Good. Be a few minutes." He went into the house.

Linda Malloy turned on me with the fire of desperate confusion in her eyes.

"What are you doing to my brother?" she demanded.

I returned her look. Though I didn't have the same fire in my gaze, I'm sure the desperation and confusion were practically the same.

"I'm trying to help," I said, "I'm trying to."

She looked at me in exasperation, wanting to attack, not being able to, wanting to trust.

"I don't think you can," she said at last. "You'll try, you'll try to help, but you won't." There was another pause filled with changing thoughts and emotions.

"You're going to hurt us."

"Probably."

"Why don't you go?"

I didn't answer.

chapter

thirty-two

The sun was making its last stand for the autumn before giving in to winter and Linda Malloy and I took advantage of it.

For me there was no debate: I wasn't welcome inside the house and I needed to wait for Lawrence Malloy. For Linda it was a matter of choice - she chose to stay with me because it gave her the opportunity to exercise her college vocabulary in a leisurely description of my failings.

We sat on the hood of my car, leaning back against the windshield, and let the heat of the sun do battle with a slightly cool autumn breeze that threatened to turn cold at any moment. The sun was winning while we waited, I in my tailor-made denim shirtsleeves, she in much more intelligently selected flannel. The heat felt deep into my bones, staying there as I allowed my eyes to close, listening to the occasional rhythms of Linda Malloy's obscenities.

I floated back into a warm memory of the '60s - she used a word that was no longer current, I corrected her - and then drifted back into the memory.

At one point, Mrs. Malloy stuck her head out of the kitchen window and caught her daughter's particularly vivid description of my lack of sexual apparatus. The cartoon popped its head back inside the window to whine a condemnation of our entire conversation, shifting the corrupting influence to me without a second's hesitation.

A moment later, Lawrence Malloy came out of the house.

"Linda," he said while getting into my car, "I don't want that kind of talk around your Momma or me."

"Yessir."

She looked at me for some sort of clue as to what I was going to say to her father, then changed the subject in her own mind.

"I meant what I said," she whispered.

"I know."

Lawrence Malloy sat in the car, next to the driver's seat, saying nothing. There was easy room for a third passenger in the front seat.

"You want to come along?" I asked Linda.

"No."

We left her walking over toward the stable.

Lawrence Malloy and I didn't have anything to say on the drive back to the pasture, but the silence was not uncomfortable. Talking probably would have been.

I stopped my car by the edge of the road and we hiked across the field to where Lawrence Malloy's pick-up was standing. Fifty yards away, atop a long mound of filled-in earth that had been a trench that morning, the bulldozer sat silent, standing guard over an empty field crisscrossed with tire tracks and a patch of scratched-out dirt that had once supported a barn. More than anything now, the land looked like it was marked out to become a housing development: bruised, waiting to be gouged. As we reached the pick-up truck, a figure came jogging from behind the bulldozer.

"Mr. Malloy!" the figure called as it approached us. "Mr. Malloy," the figure panted as it stopped in front of us. It was the operator of the machine. He was only out of breath from trying to talk and run, not from any exertion.

"I've got some papers I need you to sign." He was big, with a gentle, small-boy Southern voice.

One hand, gloved, looked huge, looked like an extension of the man's body. The other hand, un-gloved and holding the papers, was small, soft-looking, almost artificial. The artificial hand passed the papers over to Lawrence Malloy. Lawrence Malloy's hands, with the little finger missing from the right one, scratched a signature across the bottom of the top page, then returned the papers to the other mismatched pair of hands. An isolated incident among four hands, none connected with the other, the whole affair unconnected with the two men standing there.

"OK, thank you, Gene," said Malloy's father. The two men shook hands.

"I radioed-in already," Gene said. "The trailer should be here in about 'n hour, maybe less." He turned back toward his machine. "I've got to do a little maintenance work before they arrive," he added with his pleasantly rubbery twang, leaving us.

Lawrence Malloy and I watched the figure disappear behind the bulldozer, then heard the sound of over-loud tinkering on a less-than-delicate machine. The old man turned to me.

"Just saved myself a few dollars or so," he drawled, indicating the bulldozer.

"How?"

"Company machine. That piece of paper I just signed authorized the use of U.P.C. equipment for clearing a road for a lumbering operation."

"U.P.C.?"

"United Paper Company - 's who I work for. Now this is all -" Lawrence Malloy waved a maimed hand at the damaged land, "-bizness." He gave a short laugh, more breath than sound. "Y'all can see the necessity of that, right?" A pause. "Well, anyway, they're helpin' me out as they can."

"Insurance?"

"For the barn and cattle?... Covers twenty percent altogether. I quick-sold what I could today for hides, pulled out another ten percent on that. I'll get a tax write-off, of course..." He focused his eyes on the bulldozer. "It never made that much money... I don't need the money...

"I've gotta thank my neighbors."

Visions of frontier justice flashed through my mind. Suddenly I was thinking of-

Lawrence Malloy was looking at me and realized what fantasies I was conjuring up. He smiled, a real smile, at the nervousness playing across my face.

"No, I don't believe in that kind of thing," he said, growing serious at once. "But we all go to the same church on Sundays... And I'm going to speak the truth there. I want them to hear before God what they've done."

I liked his faith. It wasn't simple, I could tell that from his eyes, and it called from a man more discipline than I've ever been able to muster. But - faith, philosophy or justice - I had to take it away from him.

"They didn't do it," I said.

He looked at me without an expression that I could detect through the sun-creased lines on his face. I continued anyway:

"They didn't come here, I checked it out last night. Whoever did this had a car. Their cars were only on roads yesterday - no sign of grass, mud or feces on the tires."

Malloy's father started to fidget with his fingers. "Cleared by cow shit," he said. The uneasiness traveled steadily throughout his body, causing him to shift uncomfortably from foot-to-foot, gradually overwhelming even his face. Eyes moving from object to object, unable to concentrate, he began to look very small, unsteady. He turned quickly and scrambled into the cab of his pick-up.

An older man than I'd seen before looked down at me.

"I liked the story y'all told me last night, 'bout Davis standin' up for himself," the old, old man said. "Y'all tell it for me or the boy's mother?"

"For you," I said.

"Well, it did her the most good. Thank you." He looked over in the direction of my car. "Y'all go back and talk to Davis now," he said. "I've got to stick around here till they come to pick up the 'dozer."

Pause. Chill breeze. Smell.

"I don't know anything about what you're here for, but Davis didn't go shooting after anybody."

"You told me that last night."

"Different reasons today."

I walked to my car and drove the mile back to the Malloys' house, leaving an old man sitting in his pick-up truck. I knew from rifling through Davis Malloy's house back in Solvay that his father was all of fifty-five years old.

chapter

thirty-three

Davis Malloy was still in the kitchen when I returned. His sister was nowhere to be seen. I walked up to the kitchen door and spoke to Malloy through the screen.

"I think it's time we talked," I said. I had wanted to sound authoritative. It came out that way.

Malloy's mother, fortunately, was nowhere to be seen either. Malloy mutely appealed to the kitchen for support, then strode quickly across the room and out the door, stopping only long enough for me to get out of his way.

Increasing his pace, he walked across the yard, past all cars, and across the road, plunging into the forest with an assuredness that spoke of following a well-marked path. Though I hadn't noticed a trail when driving by, on foot I saw clearly that he was leading and I was following down a path that had been trod familiar for dozens of years.

I was excited. Despite a sense of sadness I felt betraying Davis Malloy's every step.

Didn't matter: I was more interested in what was happening than in how he felt. My stomach growled nervously and I couldn't repress a slight spring to my step.

For the first mile.

By the second mile I was considerably less springy, though still keeping pace with him. My nervous energy had given way to a rhythmic pacing.

For Davis Malloy it was different: he was driving himself - and he was in a lot worse physical condition than me. His pace was all emotion. I heard him panting, but was following a step behind and couldn't see how great the exertion was for him.

After a mile we broke out of the footpath to, for want of a better word, a car-path.

Not even developed enough to be considered a dirt road, the car-path consisted of two tire tracks cutting their way through the forest. The tracks were worn down to dirt; weedy grass sprung up in thick tufts in-between the parallel line. Davis Malloy took the right track, I pulled up parallel on the left.

The slight breeze from morning had not let up and the sweat that was saturating my shirt began to spread a clammy chill across my skin. I would have been thirsty had it been summer. Now my mouth tasted salty and my gums ached from unconsciously clenching my teeth for too long.

At the fourth mile, after an hour of walking, we stopped. My feet, long since numb from being cramped into city shoes, came to pitiful life again: they began to protest against the rough terrain we had traveled. I gave in to their argument and sat down, removing my shoes and massaging their egos.

Davis Malloy was too tired to enjoy my discomfort. I was in pain, but he was gasping, albeit as quietly as he could. He gulped a mouthful of air and said with an attempt at steadiness: "I would have driven you, but your associates have my car."

I hadn't seen his car that morning.

"How much farther?" I asked, with considerably less effort than my guide.

"Quarter mile."

I heard voices making unbusiness sounds. I looked at Malloy with a question forming.

"Just some shacks in the woods," he said. "A few people live around here. Not white. I told Golden before I brought him here. He seemed satisfied that they wouldn't give you all any trouble."

"Golden?"

I asked the question too naturally, too quickly. If I'd said the name slowly, Malloy would have let it pass as the conspiratorial rhetoric of one who "knows." But I didn't say it slowly. I asked it in such a way that Davis Malloy was half-answering before he caught on. But he was answering. And he caught on.

"E.S.C.O., Public Relations Depar-" And then he knew.

There really wasn't too much to know. I hadn't lied particularly about who I was - and if he'd listened to his sister he'd have figured out the rest. But Davis Malloy's mind had been working in one direction and had slipped me into the first logical category: that I was one of his "business associates" from E.S.T.O. or E.S.C.O. or wherever else they came from. The kind of "friend" from New York who torches barns in Alabama.

Nope, I wasn't a "friend."

"Who is Anne Malloy?" I asked.

chapter

thirty-four

Malloy was silent a minute, two. Then he began rocking gently from foot to foot.

"Oh, God," he moaned quietly, reflectively, "oh, God."

I gave him his time. I was tired, I could wait. I gave him his two minutes' silence. Then I gave him his moaning time. Then I gave him something new to think about.

"Your wife Lorraine died four years ago, your son Christy died of cancer two weeks ago, Anne Malloy was killed the day after - and you've spent the last night looking at dead cattle." It sounded cruel when I said it. I heard voices, not white, children's voices, playing children's games somewhere in the woods behind us. Anne Malloy and eighty head of cattle were murdered and children still played 'Ring Around the Rosy'. Why not? - it was a good game.

I was starting to find out something about myself: slowly and certainly, I was beginning to dislike Davis Malloy.

There is only so much dignified grief I can take. Then it becomes petrified. Oedipus' sons must have felt the same way about their noble father - not being able to deny his dignity, but unwilling to stop there like he did. So they raised a little rebellion, killing each other in the grubby process. I wanted Davis Malloy to do something. They wanted Oedipus to get up off his butt. I wanted to breath live air around him. Tragedy personified.

But he only stood, unmoving, dignified and crushed. Petrified.

"You know about the cattle?" he asked.

"I knew who didn't do it, I know now who did, and I don't know why."

"Golden said they had gotten rid of the detective."

"Bill Baeren?"

"Is that the one I hired?" Malloy looked to me for an answer.

"Yeah. Bill Baeren. Only he's not a detective: he's an attorney specializing in divorces."

Malloy looked at me uncertainly. "I had wanted a detective, he was recommended as - ?"

I didn't want to go round and round in circles, so I cut explanations short: "You hired Bill Baeren, you got a detective."

It was enough to reassure Malloy and nudge him to continue:

"He, he wasn't there, Golden said. Baeren. It was a black detective who was there, working for Baeren - the man I hired," Malloy still did not seem certain about the arrangements he himself had made. "Baeren didn't talk, they know that, Golden said."

"Bill Baeren likes a good convincing argument that can keep him out of trouble," I said, then, deciding to pretend like I knew some of the players, added: "I'm sure Golden gave him a good convincing argument."

"Golden would have talked to him, too?" Malloy asked. He looked to me for confirmation.

I'd already figured out that Bill Baeren had the backbone of an amoeba, Malloy wasn't telling me anything new in that quarter. I changed the subject.

"What about the nig- black 'detective'?" I asked: a story was beginning to take shape in the back of my mind.

"They said that a black detective was in the apartment, they ... had to kill him ... later."

So, Ray St. Johns had taken the blame for me. At least for one night, the night that counted.

"They didn't kill him, you know."

Malloy looked at me as if I were a teacher proving a parent's pet theory wrong.

"They said they killed him," he repeated, slightly defensive. "They told me that."

"They made a mistake. But they were trying."

Malloy looked offended by "their" failure.

"I came here when they told me they'd killed him," he said, still with that slightly-wounded air of being put out by having received misinformation. "He called me on the phone once. I knew they were going to kill him, so I decided to leave."

"And they followed you." I ended the story.

"What happened to the nigra-, black, detective?" Malloy asked.

"He hired me," I lied. It was getting easier daily. Come Lent I'd go to Confession, try to remember the right prayers, and wipe the slate clean.

The breeze was making me cold. I slipped on my shoes and stood up. Two thoughts were playing tag in the back of my brain. The first thought argued that if the people who had murdered Anne Malloy decided to ask Bill Baeren who he'd hired, rather than assuming that they already knew, then it wouldn't be long until they started looking for me. Especially if they bothered to delve into the experiences of a certain building superintendent by the name of Brandon. Either way, though, I was fairly safe until I got back to Syracuse.

The second thought, the one that bothered me in the immediate, concerned a place about a quarter-mile down the road. A place whose inhabitants were probably not adverse to using guns. Inhabitants who most assuredly had guns. I didn't even have a BB gun facsimile of a .45 caliber pistol. I decided to forgo further conversation with Davis Malloy in favor of flight. I needed only the answer to one more question.

"Did you see them last night?"

"Yes." The eyes looked into mine steadily. "I chased their cars thinking they were moonshiners. My daddy has had trouble with moonshiners lately."

"But you know it was them."

"I caught up with 'em," he said.

The voice was quiet, not shaking nor weak.

"They let me," he added.

I started down the car-path, away from wher-ever it was that Golden and Company were waiting. Malloy stayed rooted to where he stood.

"Come on!" I said.

"Where?" he shot back, a knowing tone to his voice.

"To the police. I don't know about anything else we can get them for, but they can rest in jail for a while for killing your father's cattle." I said it fast and logically -

- and the way Malloy was staring at something behind my back I could tell it didn't make a difference.

"They'll find us first," he said, "alone or together."

A certain nervous resemblance to panic began to stumble around inside my intestines.

By contrast, Davis Malloy seemed calmer than he had a few moments earlier. The calm of resignation.

"I'm supposed to be waiting for them in the house down the way. They'll be coming down this road before we could get past them. I thought Golden had sent you to make sure I came."

"The path? We could cut across and-"

"We can't go faster than a car. They'd be waiting at the other end. If they didn't catch up with us along the way."

Malloy said it all so matter-of-factly that I imagined he was reciting a litany well-known among the children of Chattleton: The "How To Catch Them" Te Deum.

And he was right, of course. The hum of the car's motor chimed in perfectly with the plainsong of futile escape he was droning.

chapter

thirty-five

It was a rented station wagon that came steadily down the car-path, Davis Malloy's quarry from the night before. It took the bumps smoothly, cornered without too much fish-tailing, and was obviously driven by a man who liked to let cars steer themselves to a certain extent, not a wheel-clutching over-driver. The unworried expression on the driver's face gave the impression that he had grown up driving this "road"; his suit, Syracuse pallor and hat indicated that he'd probably never seen the area before this week.

Neither had his companion in the back seat. The gentleman occupying that position maintained a constant red alert on the forest, betraying the unseen presence of some sort of firearm on his lap with a repetition of "quick-draw" starts.

Linda Malloy, sitting next to the driver, looked as if she knew the area by heart.

Not that she looked calm. When the station wagon turned into sight, she gave a heaving motion that did everything but throw-up upon recognizing us. The other two maintained their characters as the car drifted to a stop beside us.

The driver spoke with all of the Adam's Apple tension expected from a native of Buffalo, New York.

"Why don't you get in the car, Mr. Malloy?" he said.

I didn't notice the tone he used, I was too busy gritting my teeth on his pronunciation of the word "car" - he swallowed it into a painful "keer". It re-awakened my old hatred for the city of Buffalo, a prejudice started when my sister, moving there, allowed her children to join their new friends in mangling the English language. How she could have betrayed the beauty of Syracuse speech I have never understood. I have also never understood why I stood there thinking about accents while the man in the back seat of the station wagon got out and, leaning across the roof of the car, pointed a shotgun at my head.

"We told you to get into the car!" he barked with the half-assed pride of a corporal glorying in his command. The shotgun, though, carried a more compelling aura of authority. I started to comply -

- when two children stepped out of the woods behind me.

I jumped to the ground as the shotgun man jerked his weapon as if about to fire it - he was as surprised as I was by the noise behind me - and I don't know why he didn't shoot from knee-jerk overreaction. But he didn't, and the two black kids started crying, "We don'd wanna go in the car, please!"

They stepped out behind the station wagon and stood there in the middle of the car-path blubbering and afraid, precisely how I felt inside. I hoped that their bowels didn't quiver as queasily as mine were. The kids were each about seven years old, brother and sister probably, though all I could tell was that they were a boy and a girl. And they put us adults at a loss for what to do next. Finally, the shotgun man barked, "What're you doing here? Huh?!" He didn't say it too calmly and it started them crying even more.

"Don'd shoot us! Don'd shoot that man!" the little girl cried. I began to like her. Or maybe it was because I shared her sentiments.

After a moment, the driver took in the situation through his rear view mirror. Pocketing a pistol I hadn't even seen him take out, he turned quietly to Linda Malloy, nodded his head to indicated me and whispered, "Do you know his name?"

He didn't give her a chance to answer.

"Call your friend by his first name and tell him to quit horsing around."

Linda Malloy looked lost for a moment, then twisted in her seat till she could see me lying on the ground - I hadn't thought it a good idea to try hopping up. She was silent a second longer, then said, "Mark, you fucker, get in the car and quit shittin' around."

Good old Syracuse U.

I did.

The driver, meanwhile, stepped out of the car and carefully pointed his partner's shotgun skywards.

"OK," he said for the kids to hear, "you and Mark are going to quit playing cowboys and Indians. If we're going to go hunting, we'll go hunting, so stop playing around."

From my place in the back seat of the car, I couldn't resist chiming in: "That's right, Faulkner, time to hit the road!" He slammed the butt of the shotgun into my thigh as he slid onto the back seat next to me.

Davis Malloy stepped over to the side of the car, where he whispered something to his sister, then walked around to the kids.

"Y'alls daddy Ellis Tyler?" he asked.

"Umph," one of them sniffed in confirmation.

"Y'all go tell your daddy that Mr. Malloy's got some friends from up in New York down here hunting and to be careful 'cause they're not too smart with guns. Y'all tell him that I'll try to keep 'em from hurtin' anything other than a few deer, but just be careful around our place. OK?" He chucked the little boy under the chin. "S'alright," he assured them.

The silent boy nodded, the girl sniffed, "Umph-hmph," then they ran off. Malloy walked silently back to the car and got in next to his sister again.

"Thank you, Mr. Malloy," said the driver.

As we started slowly down the road, the shotgun man looked at me and asked, "Why'd you call me 'Faulkner'?"

"I read a book once. It seemed appropriate."

"Yeah. I read, too."

"Which one of you is Golden?" I asked.

Malloy's neck grew an inch thicker as it tensed.

The driver spoke from the back of his throat. "Neither of us, Mister...?" he hesitated.

"Cornell." I figured I had little left to lose. "Mark Cornell."

"Mr. Cornell. Glad to meet you. 'Mind if I call you 'Mark'?"

chapter

thirty-six

I didn't mind, but that was all he had time to say - a quarter of a mile goes past pretty quickly in a car. We found ourselves at a house, a house ending the car-path.

It was a house, too, not one of the local shacks - two-storied, white walls, green roof, veranda - not large, but comfortably sized for a family of six, as the antebellum sales brochures would say. Running water, unfortunately, not included; slaves-, er, domestics' quarters located off-premises. A hundred years ago the building had been the center of a small plantation. A fairly wide stream running behind it indicated a waterway to some larger body of water, perhaps one of the rivers feeding into Mobile Bay. Not a bad connection with civilization a century past, faster than the roads for certain.

But apparently someone had decided that lumber was a better crop than whatever had been farmed here previously. The area surrounding the house was lined with trees in such a patterned manner to indicate that fields had once existed at their bases, that the fields had been deliberately seeded. Perhaps it had been a Depression decision. The trees surrounding the house now were not more than fifteen, twenty years old - at least one crop of lumber had been harvested already - so maybe the decision had been a profitable one. At any rate, the Malloys had kept up the house with fresh coats of whitewash and fairly new roofing. It wasn't a showplace, but it beat out half the neighborhood in terms of construction. The only thing missing was the touch of human habitance. The man standing in the doorway waiting for us didn't quite have enough of the human being in him to add that touch.

He disappeared into the house as the station wagon came to a halt.

Without any effort or coercion, the driver and his partner casually herded our Malloy-Cornell party toward the house, walking ahead as if they lived there, and simply opening the door for us, not even waiting to see if we followed. Of course, the shotgun that Faulkner carried didn't leave much room for doubt about where we'd be going.

Now under the watchful eye of the man who had so recently disappeared from the doorway, they handled the transfer with a certain grace that had been lacking from our initial encounter. On reflection, I realized that I had received this type of treatment before: upon entering the office of the E.S.T.O. manager for my apartment complex. E.S.T.O. must have a training course in Client Relations, I imagined.

I couldn't help liking the man who had to be Golden. For one thing, he talked to Davis Malloy the way I'd been aching to for the past two days.

"Dave, you bastard, you've been one asshole as it is! Now what the hell do you have going on?"

Golden moved briskly and businesslike, without threat, without friendliness, and without any hint of crudity in the language he was using. He was genuinely angry and genuinely concerned - not playing a role like shotgunner-cum-corporal Faulkner standing by the door, nor coolly masking his feelings as the driver had. When Malloy answered his question with another of his dignified looks of silent tragedy, Golden stopped himself from starting to shout and, visibly calming himself, concluded the situation decisively: "OK. We'll find that out on the way home, Dave. Right now I want the papers and your signature."

Suddenly the living room of the hundred year-old house became a business office. The driver pulled a briefcase from behind the front door. Setting it upon a dining table, from elsewhere he produced a portable typewriter and sheaves of paper, complete with carbons, an ink eraser and a razor blade for correcting carbon copy errors. At the other end of the table, the shotgun was placed next to an ink pad and a rubber stamp. A small Notary Public's raised-seal press appeared in the center of things.

Golden glanced through the handful of papers Malloy produced from his jacket pocket, then began dictating his own name, then Malloy's name, a serial number of some sort, and the date to the driver, who promptly typed the information onto some New York State tax forms. Finally, Golden held out a pen to Malloy, who signed where indicated. Golden then signed the same papers himself, gave the papers to his nearby Notary Public and took them back when signed and stamped: whatever their business was, it was over.

Golden flopped down into a fairly comfortable-looking sofa and didn't invite any of us to join him.

"Go on, sit down if you want," he said, indicating the less desirable locations. "I have to leave in a minute, but let's see what we can while we can."

"Hi, I'm Mark Cornell," I said.

"I'm Steve Golden. You know - ?" he indicated his friends.

"I didn't catch their names, no," I answered, rubbing a bruised thigh, "but it doesn't matter: I'm lousy at remembering names."

"'Got a point there," Golden agreed. He turned to Linda who, like me, was still standing dumbly in the middle of the room. Her brother was posing tragically by the table. "OK, Miss Malloy. What happened?"

The word she was about to say would not have produced a happy effect, but she happened to glance at her brother before saying it and opted for an "I don't know" instead.

"You probably don't," said Golden, "but your brother said you were with him last night, and I have to check these things out."

"What about last night?" Linda cried, her eyes filled with a confusion bordering on pain.

Golden leaned forward, looking her squarely in the face. Then he lied very well.

"Your brother called us last night. He told us that someone had ruined your father's farm and that he needed help. Protection. Only he left us here this morning and I'm afraid we got worried. That's why I blew up at your brother."

On second thought, it wasn't a very good lie, as Golden could see when he'd finished telling it. Though it succeeded in confusing Linda, it needed something more to convince her. He called over to Malloy.

"Davis, why don't you take your sister outside and explain the situation to her. Mark and I will clear some other things up. OK?"

Linda Malloy didn't wait for her brother's reply, but walked out of the room saying, "I'll be waiting by the car." Her brother followed.

Golden turned to me, off-handedly confiding: "Davis sure messed things up. What are you doing here?"

"I was hired by a black guy up in Syracuse to find out why somebody is trying to kill him."

"And?"

"You think he saw who killed Anne Malloy."

Steve Golden stared down at the floor, reflective and priestlike. "Was that her name?" he said quietly. "I'll have to ask Davis about it."

One minute. Two. With a nice, comfortable silence. Then Golden, still looking at the floor, tossed out the matter-of-fact question:

"Did he?"

"No. He was there when she came. He left before anybody else arrived.'You do it?"

"No."

"'You know who did?"

Golden's two friends looked uneasily at me. Steve Golden simply smiled a smile that said he was thinking of other things.

"Do you know what it's all about?" he asked at last.

"It has to do with blackmail," I said. "A certain electronics expert-turned-apartment superintendent has led me to believe that you folks at E.S.T.O. and E.S.C.O. probably make your business deals in some less than aboveboard ways. Like snooping, tape recording, et cetera...."

Golden's expression took on a vague, searching blankness. "Oh - that," he said dismissively, orientation returning to his eyes. "You may be right. I never really looked into it. I don't think so, though, to tell you the truth. I think it was more to prevent blackmail, like old Davis was up to."

"Prevent blackmail?"

Golden looked at me a little incredulously. Then his face lit up. "Ah!, you didn't see this."

He took the papers from out of his coat pocket. Filled with legal jargon and the usual New York State tax form confusion, the documents added up to one thing: a transfer of property, Belle Fredonia property.

"Two years ago," Golden began, looking over my shoulder at the papers, "Davis Malloy received a year-end bonus of five thousand dollars - a bonus carrying the verbal suggestion that he use it to purchase some land upstate. Very legal and very his. The only request accompanying the bonus was that if ever he received a telephone call asking him not to visit his land, he would do so for a few days. OK, no problems.

"Until a month ago. I offered to buy Dave's land from him, an arrangement he was also suggested to expect. Only -"

Golden looked to me to finish the sentence and I took a shot at what seemed like the impending glitch:

"- Only: Dave didn't want to sell."

"I offered him a pretty good profit on the land, too." Golden's eyebrows drew together, worried. He looked for something among the papers and, reassured as he found it, said without looking up: "And so, we're here."

He looked over at me. "You know where you fit in?" he asked.

"Um-hmm." I wanted a bathroom.

"Malloy planned a double-cross of some sort, hiring a detective to keep an eye on the situation in the apartment and keep you-"

"I wasn't there."

"-keep your business associates," I corrected, "from trying to do anything. You - they - went to Salina Street expecting to transfer the deed?"

"People went there with that in mind," was the grunted response. Then Golden continued to complain:. "It was not the first time Dave had tried a stall. But he was told it would be the last time."

"Yeah, only he tried anyway, maybe this time

putting a little threat behind his stall." Golden nodded his head in a way that told me how personally annoyed he was by Davis Malloy's actions. "What does a man like Malloy want more than money?" I asked.

"I never asked him," said Golden. He was starting to look like he wasn't worried anymore.

But I knew more, and I wanted to get it out.

"Malloy made a mistake, obviously, when he thought you could be pressured and-"

"I wasn't there," Golden repeated.

"I don't feel like playing diplomat anymore," I snarled, feeling more like a scared victim than the tough, inquiring mind I hoped was coming off. "You had to be there to sign the papers, I saw that today. Besides, what does it matter? You made your share of mistakes, today wasn't the first." I took a breath and went back to my story.

"Malloy hired a detective so that he could throw around a name, hoping you wouldn't know it was only a divorce detective. He sent a woman so that there'd be another witness. He made the mistake of thinking that you'd let a detective stand in your way. So you killed the girl to get Malloy off his ass, then you went after the detective, who had been seen leaving the apartment." I paused for air. I forget to breathe sometimes. But I wasn't through talking.

"I got a question. Mind if I ask it?"

"'Depends," said Golden.

"Did Malloy try to play on your sympathy about his kid dying of cancer?"

"Yes."

"I thought so. And he sent a girl in his place and hired someone else to protect her."

"Then he came running here."

"Yeah."

Golden asked, "You said we made a mistake?"

"You didn't kill the black guy, the detective."

"Now he's hired you to tell us that he didn't see anything?"

I figured "what-the-hell?" and told them: "He didn't hire me. He wasn't the detective. I am."

Well, now they knew.

"I'm the guy that saw Anne Malloy die."

chapter

thirty-seven

If I'd expected a big reaction I would have been disappointed. Steve Golden looked at me with mild curiosity and the other two - the driver and Faulkner - didn't look in our direction at all. Did they already know or what?, I thought. Then I answered my own question with the obvious - they didn't care anymore. I was dead, so whatever I knew couldn't affect them. The thought did nothing for my nerves, but got my self-righteousness worked up even more than it had been. I attacked verbally.

"Tell me," I demanded, "is the land worth killing for? What's there?"

Golden looked at me vaguely again.

"I wouldn't know," he admitted. "I've never cared to ask. I don't think Dave knows either. It's better not to know - but then," he looked at me a little pedantically, "it's too late for you to learn that."

I pretended that I didn't hear what he said and asked, "Why is Davis Malloy still alive?"

"Because he's a good chemist, Mark, E.S.C.O. needs his services. Besides, for public relations - my specialty - it's good to have an example available. It keeps people's ambitions within limits."

I shot back quickly, "You didn't even ask what Malloy's ambitions were."

"Well, you see Mark, there's always the question of timing: I think it's even possible that Dave has a bigger future ahead of him as a result of this little trouble."

He saw the look of disgust plastered across my face and, looking as if he was an adultering parent trying to explain his philandering to a disappointed son, began to elaborate:

"You have to understand that trouble like you've been witness to is not our main interest. Basically, we want to make our profits from real estate or, in my case with E.S.C.O., from chemical processing. This business with Dave Malloy is totally unrelated to his talents as a chemist. You know, I didn't even know Dave until a month ago - I'm P.R., he's chemicals - and I'm personally in no position to help his career. What do you think? With thirty thousand employees - thirty thousand - do you think I can know everyone?"

He waited for an answer. I gave him one.

"How many do you need to know?"

"Not many," he said casually, but still earnestly. "One, maybe two percent, that's all that's ever necessary for control. I don't even think it's one percent, that would be over a hundred, wouldn't it?"

"Three hundred," said the driver.

"Three hundred," I said. "That's a lot of people. Must be a lot of crime in Syracuse these days."

"We're an open book, Mark, anybody can check that out for themselves. But... Well, this morning Dave's father used a company bulldozer, didn't he? The difference between using a company car for private purposes and between using the company payroll for sub-organizational purposes is not that great."

"As in Davis Malloy's land-buying bonus."

"Um-hmm."

"Why do you do it?"

"Why?" Golden looked surprised at the question. So was I. It was simpler than what I'd intended to ask. But it was what I wanted to know.

Strangely, after musing on it for a few seconds, Golden took the question seriously, albeit with a slight, shrugging, half-laugh.

"Every man has his own reasons for anything he does. I suppose my interest is job security." He gave another half-laugh, self-consciously. "Job security in a profession not known for that characteristic. I am a Public Relations man," he added rather defensively.

"As for Dave, you can try to figure him out for yourself: I can't." The admission was straightforward - undercut a moment later by a sly wink: "I think I can guess, though, why he'll be with us for the future."

"Why?"

"Well, Mark, he's implicated in a number of illegal activities, and I think he's afraid of going to jail for them."

Golden looked at me with a 'you understand' shrug, adding, "And, then, Davis Malloy is also one of the conspirators in your murder."

chapter

thirty-eight

We sat waiting for Davis and Linda Malloy to come back into the house, an uncomfortable silence hanging like cotton between us. I had nothing more to say or ask, especially about the details of my future. Golden, having made his point in his own roundabout, comfortable fashion, was content to busy himself with checking out his travel arrangements in a notebook extracted from a coat pocket. His friends, still doing the small detail paperwork of the land transaction, were re-reading for errors. I tried to hear the voices of Davis and Linda Malloy.

There was nothing to hear. I supposed that they had said all that they needed to say, now they were - what?

Now they were coming in the front door. As soon as he saw them, Golden stood up.

"Everything all right, Dave?" he asked.

"Yes."

"Well, we've gotta get to Birmingham by five today if we want to arrive in Syracuse before tomorrow night. 'Think we can make it?"

"Maybe."

"Let's try, OK?" Golden turned to his friends and scooped up the papers. "I'll go with Dave and his sister: we can drop her off at home and he can say his good-byes there." He turned to me and said as if doing me a favor: "I'll pick up your car from their place and meet you at the airport, Mark. You can ride in the other car, it's got a tape deck and I think you'll like the tunes."

"Any flute music?"

"No," a frown.

"Oh, well. Where's the second car? I didn't see it when we came in."

Another frown: "Around the back."

I decided to take a chance: "You want to come with us, Linda? I'd like to say good-bye, too."

A third frown: "Mark -"

"Yes, I would," said Linda.

Davis Malloy stood there, watching.

Golden didn't miss a beat. "OK, Dave, let's go then." He looked over at his friends: "Change of plans," he said, going out the door. "Make it two. See you in Salt City." He stopped just outside the door. "Mark," he said, looking in through the screen, "I forgot: I'll need your car keys. Dave, will you get them? I'll go warm up my car."

Linda Malloy looked at her brother as he walked over and took the keys I held out for him.

"Davis," she asked, "am I in trouble?"

His face handsome and tragic, voice low yet clear, Davis Malloy regarded his sister unflinchingly. "Yes," he said, turned, and walked out of the house. A moment later we heard Golden's car drive off.

"Hmmm," I heard the driver mutter as he took his pistol out from somewhere again.

I had a feeling that it was time for me to die.

I tried to put some distance between Linda and myself, to keep her out of the line of fire, hoping that maybe she could run for it.

I forgot to tell Linda my idea, however: as I slid away from her, she slid right back next to me. We probably would have skated halfway around the room like that if Faulkner hadn't decided to level his shotgun at a point mid-way between the two of us.

"If you move again I'll shoot off your right arm and her left arm," he said with experienced certainty. Faulkner didn't look half as nervous as he had in the car. Maybe it was because we weren't surrounded by trees. Maybe it was because he just felt comfortable in a house.

"But we don't want you to look like you've been shot," his friend added. "When they find your bodies in the ashes, it'll look like you two were just shacked-up together, maybe a little drunk, and burned to death by accident." He pronounced the words 'aeshes', 'sheacked' and other atrocities. It annoyed the hell out of me.

Linda did not move. I didn't either. Faulkner put down his shotgun and walked over to where we were standing. He motioned to Linda to sit. She remained frozen, standing. Then his friend with the pistol came over and pulled her down to the sofa. He joined Faulkner standing in front of me.

"Of course, you'll be dead first," he added as an afterthought, and raised the pistol, butt first, over my head.

I was too scared to move, even though I wanted to with all my might. I watched as he brought the gun down. I felt my left ear burn with pain as if it were being torn off, and an explosion that immediately became a numb ringing filled my head as it struck.

And then I didn't feel anything but anger.

He hadn't hit hard enough to knock me out, all he'd done was release the last block to an anger that had been bottled up for weeks. And now I didn't even think. My head was numbed from the blow, but I was wide awake, conscious. And angry! I instinctively grabbed at the gunman's face with only one thought in my mind - to rip it off!

If I surprised myself, I surprised them even more. For the first second Faulkner stood there watching as I brought two fists into the cheeks of his partner, then grabbed what was underneath them. By the second second I was yelling at the top of my lungs and throwing that face into Faulkner's face, ramming my head into the whole conglomeration of faces before we three split apart and found ourselves sprawled at opposite corners of the room.

I didn't even think to worry about the pistol the one guy was still holding: I grabbed the nearest thing that could be picked up - I think it was a chair - and started swinging it like a bat at their bodies, sending them back down to the floor before they could rise half to their feet again. Whatever it was I was swinging was strong: when it finally did break across one of Faulkner's arms, I heard a non-wood crack that sickened my stomach.

But not enough to stop me hitting them. Or swinging. I stood in the middle of the room blindly scything dangerous half-circles as they ran past me out the door. It was only Linda's screaming "Mark! Get the shotgun!" that made me stop. I threw my weapon down, ran to the table, grabbed the shotgun and stood there waiting.

If they had come back into the house at that minute, they could have shot me and it would have been over: I couldn't think and I couldn't move. But I guess they couldn't, either. I really didn't care what they were doing, though, and if it hadn't been for Linda grabbing the shotgun from my inert paws and blasting a hole through the screen door to let them know that we were waiting for them, they probably would have come charging back in and shot me. All I knew at that moment was that I couldn't focus my eyes and that if I didn't hold onto something I was going to start shaking and never stop. I stumbled over to the sofa, sat down holding myself tight, and started shivering. I had the worst headache in my existence.

I was still shivering five minutes later when I joined Linda at a window and took the gun from her. I couldn't stop the shaking, but I wasn't afraid anymore. I didn't feel sick, despite the headache. I felt happy. I wanted to fight again. I wanted to whup them. I wanted to get killed.

"Mark, if you walk out that door they'll shoot you in the head."

I hadn't thought about that. I had a shotgun, they should be afraid of me - that was what I had been thinking. Only Linda had not lost sight of the important fact: I had only one shot, they had a pistol with several shots to it and maybe another weapon. In addition, they could wait out there until nightfall and then come after us. We could only wait.

Siege.

It was one o'clock in the afternoon. Steve Golden and Davis Malloy had left us only fifteen minutes before. We had five hours of daylight remaining, an hour of dusk after that. I looked out the window and didn't see a thing.

"Check the back door and windows," I said.

"Padlocked. They always are."

"Maybe your brother opened them!" I said with too much emphasis.

She didn't even notice. She also didn't do what I ordered.

"He couldn't," she answered tersely, "Daddy lost the key a year ago."

We waited an hour, two. My head pounded, ear throbbing and eyes dangerously near to losing focus any time I came close to relaxing. Linda wasn't in much better shape, starting to shake from the adrenaine rush a few moments into our wait and then, when that had drained away, from delayed emotion. I put one arm around her and we were a St. Vitus Dance poster couple until shared body warmth and emotional support let us settle into a miserable semblance of tolerable, alert discomfort.

The only consolation I had was that it started to rain, the cool breeze of the early day finally having brought some clouds with it. Raining on everything outside, including the now-shotgunless Faulkner and his pistol-packing pal. Every few minutes I ran from window to window, checking to see that they were still locked and that no one was lurking beneath them. After awhile, I walked from window to window: as Linda also pointed out, the heavy screens covering each pane of glass were virtually glued into their frames by virtue of several coats of whitewash casually slopped onto the outside walls every Spring. It would take a few minutes hard work with a screwdriver to loosen the seams. Except for the front door, Linda and I were safe from any rushed-in attack.

Except for, maybe, the fact that a bullet could go through mesh screen and glass as easily as a knife through whipped margarine. Linda pulled down the dusty Venetian blinds of each window and closed them : we could still look out, but nobody was going to be taking potshots from seeing us inside.

They never approached their car.

Or maybe they had been there first, then left when Linda fired the shotgun, taking what they needed.

What did they need? A doctor, I hoped. Probably only band-aids and bullets. I stomach made a vocal protest that it could have used some food after the third hour, but I found out I was too nervous to eat when Linda scavenged through the kitchen and found some leftovers from last night's guests' dinner.

For all the importance of my life being at stake, I still felt bored.

Just before dusk, in the last of the sunlight, the rain cleared up.

The air took on a wet, cold clarity that sunset only lanced here and there.

From a point not more than a hundred yards away from the house, there came the spastic crackle of several guns being fired - rifles - a sound that lasted all of five seconds. My heart tried to jump out of my mouth but was stopped by my teeth.

I moved closer to the front door, ready. I could see out on a wider range of forest now and, hopefully, it was too dark inside the house to be seen.

Nothing moved and the shadows grew darker outside. Soon they would be as invisible out there as were we inside. Linda moved up to the door next to me, holding a kitchen knife, ready to strike from that side.

The air felt deadly clean. I took several deep breaths, shivering at the winter in its bite.

I needed a jacket. Linda had a light one on, but was shivering anyway. Searching around the house quickly, our eyes constantly on the front door, the shotgun always pointed there, we found a couple of heavy wool blankets. Giving one to Linda, I wrapped the other around myself, looking less like a noble Indian than a U.N.I.C.E.F.-poster refugee. Infused with a blanket-inspired inner warmth and the perception of an increasing exterior darkness, however, I felt a growing sense of boldness.

After a brief consultation with Linda, I slipped out the front door and laid myself flat across the narrow porch. I assumed I would be almost invisible, especially with the dark blanket pulled over my head like a hood. I crouched low behind the sights of the shotgun - and waited - looking in the direction the gunshots had come from. The cold rain water that had beaded up on the porch soaked through the front of my shirt.

A man stepped out of the woods -

I took a deep breath, afraid to use my one shot too soon.

- a man I had seen lying on a rug watching color television the night before.

He carried a sportsman's poncho raincoat and walked directly at the house.

"Miz Malloy!" he called out. "Yerr daddy said y'all kin come home now!"

He stepped up to the porch and tossed me the raincoat. "Give this to Miz Malloy," he said.

Then he held out his hand. I started to tentatively hold out mine to shake it, but he waved-off the gesture. "We gotta lose this," he said, indicating the shotgun. I gave it to him.

Linda turned on a kerosene lamp inside the living room and came to the door. Standing just inside the screen, she addressed the man with the simple identification: "'Mister McKyle."

"Miz Malloy."

A moment later she added: "Thank you."

McKyle shrugged his uncomfortable acceptance of the sentiment before adding: "Y'all kin tell Davis thet we don'd like people thinkin' we killed his daddy's cattle, not by burnin'm in a barn."

chapter

thirty-nine

The keys to the rented station wagon parked behind the house were sitting on the living room table. I hadn't noticed them before. So Steve Golden's "business associates" probably never got into the car after all.

It didn't matter. They'd still had a pistol and it only took one bullet to kill a man.

I swept up their belongings, dumped them into the rear seat of the car, and sat behind the steering wheel to wait for Linda. I was still wrapped in my blanket. Linda joined me, after talking with her bootleg-*meister* neighbor McKyle for a few minutes, then she directed us back to her house.

My car was gone, of course: Golden had taken it to Birmingham.

No one was home at the Malloys' place. Linda got out of the car, said "Good-bye," and went into the dark house. She didn't turn on a light, but moved about inside the house with familiarity.

If she was moving about.

I'd like to think that she was looking out a window at me as I drove away. But I doubted it. We had hardly said a word all afternoon. Not since the time, arm draped over her shaking shoulder and waiting for two men to rush in and kill us, I tried to tell her what had happened in Syracuse.

"Don't," was all she said.

Now she had said her good-bye to me and that was all that was necessary. I left.

I left her to explain the past two days to her parents, knowing that Davis Malloy would come through it all clean to at least one pair of ears. I imagined the old man would become better neighbors with the Mc-Kyles, take their word for the goings-on - and their version of 'Walker Red - and lose his son somewhere in the distilled oblivion.

My car was sitting in the short-term parking lot outside the airport in Birmingham - I found it without too much trouble, keys still in the ignition, door unlocked. I paid the fine for over-parking the time limit, and left a rented station wagon (with a great tape deck) abandoned on a side street half a block away from the main terminal.

I made it to Syracuse in two days of long driving. I went to the first hardware store I could find, bought a bolt lock, then went to my apartment, fixed the lock to the door and fell asleep for another two days.

It wasn't a deep sleep. Most of the time I just lay with my eyes closed and not an intelligent thought in my mind. I rested better that way, without troublesome dreams.

chapter

forty

The skyline of Syracuse has become varied in the past five years by several buildings purporting to be skyscrapers. The once-standard four- and five-story terrain now boasts several twenty-to-forty-floor edifices, presenting a not-unattractive silhouette against the beautiful Syracuse sunsets. The new buildings are mainly glass and metal structures. Occasionally, on foggy or rainy nights, sometimes even in the snow, the eerie effect is created of a life above the world when, briefly, through a hole in the dense weather, one can see an entire floor of lighted windows hovering overhead without any apparent connection to the earth below.

The nostalgic predecessors of them all are the two square towers comprising the MONY Center. The first of the really big ones built in the heart of Syracuse, the MONY buildings can still be seen from the ridge of the valley that encircles Syracuse, flashing temperature and time readings every five seconds consecutively. Atop one of the towers, I never remember which, is a blinking star: colored red, white, yellow and green, the star broadcasts a particular color when the weather is clear, when a storm is approaching, when there is a storm, and when it snows. Again, I can never remember which color is which, but every morning I get up and look at the tower to see what the day will be like. So do thousands of other people as well. The time is more popular, though. On the days when the MONY building is off by five minutes, so too is half of the Salt City.

Various companies rent offices in the MONY buildings, several rent entire floors. Graced with excellent parking facilities, the MONY Center is the most prestigious location in Syracuse. It was only natural, then, that in one tower of the MONY Center an entire level was rented by the Eastern States Title Operators, while, in the other tower, the Eastern States Chemical Organization occupied similarly extensive administrative lodgings. The twelfth and eighth floors, respectively. I was standing in the offices of the eighth floor.

It didn't surprise me to find that Mr. Stephan Golden, E.S.C.O. Public Relations Department, had been transferred to the state capitol offices in Albany. A promotion to governmental PR liaison. Mr. Golden was, of course, still residing in Syracuse (DeWitt, actually: which I knew from the telephone book, and his ex-reception secretary knew from her Rolodex files, though neither of us were inclined to share that personal knowledge with the other), but only until he settled his personal affairs and relocated his family to Albany. He was commuting to Albany for four days at a time. Although he was gone at the present moment, the ex-sec informed me, Steve Golden would return on Friday if I cared to make an appointment.

I did not care to make an appointment.

I was surprised, though, about the rise in status Golden was enjoying. Apparently news about the mishmash down in Alabama had not filtered north to the upper echelons yet? Or did corporate criminal management suffer the same Peter Principles of executive advancement as its more benign counterparts. Had Steve Golden's promotion brought him to his level of incompetence yet?

Probably, instead, a fine example of P.Y.A. was at work - Protect Your Ass. Golden did his job, I could imagine the argument going, he brought back the title transfers; it was those fuck-ups Faulkner and What's-His-Name dead down in Swamptown, U.S.A. who screwed the pooch from there. A convenient interpretation, if you were Steve Golden. It all depended upon who Stevie's mentors were - and what Davis Malloy said.

I began to understand why Steve Golden felt there was so much promise in Dave Malloy's future. Siamese twins had looser symbiotic bonds.

Still, no Steve Golden to visit this week.

I had better luck when I asked about the corporate whereabouts of Davis Malloy: he came to the MONY Center offices almost daily for conferences with his immediate supervisor on developments in the E.S.C.O. labs. In fact, same kindly secretary offered, he would be in today at about noon if I cared to wait. I cared to and went out into the lobby.

A large picture window in the E.S.C.O. lobby looked out onto the MONY Plaza, a concrete flatland eighty feet down below without any particular characteristic other than the fact that it is always crowded. The picture window wasn't particularly unusual, either, since 90% of the MONY building appears to be windows. I think it keeps the workers distracted - life is always a little more interesting outside the glass than in. I found a comfortable-looking chair near the window and pulled it closer. The chair was less comfortable than its design had indicated, but I was feeling lazy and stayed sitting. I watched the ebb and flow of the crowd below.

Crowds are never solid. Sometimes they surge in a mass of ten followed by a space occupied by only three or four people. Normally there are small islands of stationary bodies even in the midst of the most hurrying crowds. At one point, the crowd swept past and left three men standing almost alone in a corner of the plaza.

One of them was Davis Malloy.

I sat back in my chair and decided to watch how Davis Malloy lives his daily life. I had only seen him in crisis situations; I was curious. Did he wave his arms excitedly? Perhaps he stood stock still? I wondered who his friends down there were, watched them almost swept away by the passing tide of yet another mass of people. Davis Malloy, his back to a small, ungrowing tree, did not move.

It was an Indian Summer day, probably the last one before winter gained total control over Syracuse. Although it had already snowed once that autumn, people now took advantage of the respite to walk about clad only in sweaters and light jackets. Davis Malloy wore a suede sports coat that looked just right for a Solvay bar drinker. I made myself comfortable in the uncomfortable chair and allowed the sunlight to make me feel almost hot.

Again, there was a break in the crowd. Davis Malloy left his fellow conversants and started toward the entrance to the MONY building I was sitting in. Though walking in a straight line, he soon had to curve to avoid another islet of stationary talkers. Half-circling around them, he was suddenly face-to-face with one group of walkers and de facto lead cow heading a second group. He swerved to the right and his group did likewise. Now he was walking parallel to the front entrance of the building, in the midst of a directionless crowd. Forcing his way left, he tried pushing toward the door when, for no noticeable reason, the crowd disappeared, leaving him pushing against nothing, walking alone in the middle of the MONY Plaza.

For a second Malloy seemed self-conscious about having no one to push, but before he walked twenty yards he had side-stepped several groups leaving the building. He did it smoothly, without effort, as he had the entire crossing of the plaza.

But he still could not get in. The revolving doors held back a crowd of people waiting to be processed inside. Almost immediately below my window, Davis Malloy had to stand and wait his turn to be pushed in. I turned my head sideways against the glass to see him.

If the window had been open, I could have spit on his head. I thought about it: it would have been more fun than talking to him.

Suddenly I didn't want to talk to him. Not in the MONY building, not in the E.S.C.O. offices. Not with the little head eight stories below me who I wanted to spit on.

When Davis Malloy arrived on the eighth floor of the MONY building and its E.S.C.O. offices, he did not find me waiting for him.

chapter

forty-one

Saturday. Twenty days after a red-headed woman had been thrown out of a window. Eight days after fifty head of cattle were butchered in a field at night. Seven days after two men whose names I didn't care to learn disappeared from the face of the earth. And three days after I had watched a tiny human figure cut through the crowd at the MONY Plaza.

Saturday.

Afternoon.

And I was in Solvay.

And I was in Solvay.

I sat in my car with the windows closed tight, watching a silent movie. Actually, I was waiting for the movie to begin. Though it was a clear, cold November afternoon - sun shining and all - there were no people to see. No reason to do yard work: the ground was rock-hard frozen, snow would be descending on us any day now, and all of the autumn leaves had been scraped away weeks before. The trees stood naked.

'Too cold to go casually walking down to the store, either: car time of year. A few ripples of heat escaped from the tops of houses with fireplaces, the only signs that the neighborhood was not a ghost town. No chimney at the Malloy residence.

But Davis Malloy was at home, I knew that. Parked three houses down the block from his house, I could see his car in the driveway.

In the past week I had learned quite a few things about how the world worked. A certain Russian-speaking black-hued police detective had explained the world to me - a world without material witnesses, without records, without legitimate complainants, without names and dates and figures... A world that was untouchable to an ordinary Russian-speaking black-hued police detective man.

I started my engine and let it idle, turning on the heater to warm up my legs.

Detective Lieutenant Anderson had explained to me how companies with open books could not possible be linked with crime. Conspiracies, at any rate, were simply a national obsession ever since Watergate a couple of years ago - and anyway, those types of investigation required political decisions, political acts designed to provoke a scandal (if your party was out-of-office) or avoid a scandal (if in) or (in mixed circles) at least ride out the political storm that would inevitably ensue. But was it inevitable? Open books and tenuous links - with no legally admissible evidence in-between. When industries and innocent jobs are at stake, the beliefs of an individual take second place.

I released the emergency brake, shifted into first gear, and drifted slowly down the street.

Of course, Anderson did not do all of the explaining. For my part there was mention of certain extenuating circumstances concerning a black gunman by the name of Ray St. Johns, serendipitous events unfortunately based on individual interpretation. Nothing that could be put on paper. However, Lieutenant Anderson considered the interpretation not without merit, especially upon inspection of St. Johns' shotgun-racked premises, and ordered the release of the "gunman" upon payment of damages to repair shop owners' windows.

I stopped the car in front of Malloy's house. It's a 1965 Mercury Comet. 'Gets lousy mileage in these days of 95 cent-per-gallon gas and not-too-long ago lines to buy it at any price. Great heater, though. It was cold outside.

There was also mention from Lieutenant Anderson of a possible criminal violation in connection with my bank account transactions recently, or lack thereof. I suggested that Bill Baeren had assured me he would cover any overdrafts I made. When called by the bank, he did not recall the offer. Lieutenant Anderson interviewed him personally, suggesting that Bill should try remembering his obligations. He did.

The cold sunlight made Malloy's white house look sterile and pale. The worn grass was brown, ash-like.

I leaned against the steering wheel, causing the horn to blare out.

It sounded loud from inside my car. It sounded louder outside the car. I didn't feel like leaning against the wheel, so I sat back. Immediately the sound stopped.

But I straightened my arm against the steering wheel and the sound started again.

I kept the motor running, rather than wear down the battery. The sound stayed loud and strong. I had to switch arms several times because it was tiring keeping the horn blowing, but the sound remained unbroken.

Within a minute, however, I didn't hear the sound. Not consciously. It was merely a background to the silent movie unfolding before me. Up and down the neighborhood street doors opened and heads (sometimes whole bodies) popped out to see what the ruckus was all about. I pulled the car into Malloy's driveway, my arm still rigidly on the horn. Most of the heads and bodies popped back inside again, but a few stayed put, anxious to see what jerk was disturbing their afternoon football game (S.U. versus Army, away - I had tickets, damn!). I stayed in the car and disappointed them.

Finally, Davis Malloy opened his door.

The strong-featured man came striding out to see what was happening in front of his house. He was halfway across his yard when I lifted my hand and the sound stopped. He stopped as well. I didn't. I opened my car door, stood up alongside it, and asked:

"Who is Anne Malloy?"

He didn't say a word. Quickly and forcefully, Davis Malloy returned to his house, slamming the door behind him.

I sat back in my car, closing the door with considerably less nervousness than Malloy had his. I pulled out a book, leaned it against the steering wheel and, pushing the car horn at the same time, began reading.

It was a dull book and I found my mind wandering. I wondered how long it would take the police to arrive. I wondered how many times I would have to repeat stunts like this and tell my story before people started doing something.

I knew some people would start doing things right away, not necessarily things I would appreciate.

That was why I had decided to cultivate a close literary relationship with Lieutenant Anderson: I wanted those people to know I had friends...

I put down the book I wasn't reading and picked up my copy of *The Possessed* that Anderson had returned.

In Russian.

Old Alphabet.

I tried not to think of a woman who I had seen get thrown out of a sixth story window.

the end

* * * * * * * * * * * * * *

* * * * * * * *

* * *

*

DANGER
LIVE ANIMAL

Robert C. Fleet was born in Tyler, Texas, where a famous actress was once his babysitter. Never recovering from that experience, he went into show business himself - as an actor with a Chinese theater troupe in New York City. Later marrying into Polish nobility, he taught himself that language while living in Inglewood, California. Meanwhile he paid for the sin of not taking math in college by ghost-writing a mathematics textbook as his first professional writing gig. These experiences have led him to live and work in several countries as either a writer, actor or filmmaker. He has been owned by several animals.

www.ingramcontent.com/pod-product-compliance
Lightning Source LLC
Chambersburg PA
CBHW020243180626
46810CB00006B/2334